Where the Ghosts Are

A Guide to Nova Scotia's Spookiest Places

By Steve Vernon

NIMBUS
PUBLISHING LTD.
—— NIMBUS.CA ——

Nimbus Publishing Limited
3660 Strawberry Hill Street, Halifax, NS, B3K 5A9
(902) 455-4286 nimbus.ca

Printed and bound in Canada
NB1361

Editors: Lexi Harrington & Emily MacKinnon
Cover & interior illustrations: Alex MacAskill, Midnight Oil Print & Design House
Cover and interior design: Grace Laemmler Design

Library and Archives Canada Cataloguing in Publication

Vernon, Steve, author
Where the ghosts are : a guide to Nova Scotia's spookiest places / Steve Vernon.

Includes bibliographical references and index.
Issued in print and electronic formats.
ISBN 978-1-77108-699-8 (softcover).—ISBN 978-1-77108-700-1 (HTML)

1. Haunted places—Nova Scotia. 2. Ghosts—Nova Scotia.
3. Ghost stories, Canadian (English)—Nova Scotia. I. Title.

BF1472.C3V475 2018   133.109716   C2018-902935-8
                                    C2018-902936-6

Canadä   NOVA SCOTIA   Canada Council   Conseil des arts
                                        for the Arts   du Canada

Nimbus Publishing acknowledges the financial support for its publishing activities from the Government of Canada, the Canada Council for the Arts, and from the Province of Nova Scotia. We are pleased to work in partnership with the Province of Nova Scotia to develop and promote our creative industries for the benefit of all Nova Scotians.

MIX
Paper from
responsible sources
FSC® C103113

To Marjorie Chatelois, my mother, my friend,
and the person who always believed in my writing.
This book is dedicated to you, Mom.

TABLE OF CONTENTS

Section 3: Northern Shore & Cape Breton

Section 4: Eastern Shore

Section 5: Central & Halifax

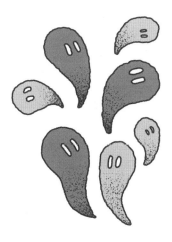

Introduction

I N 2009 I SAT DOWN AND WROTE A BOOK ENTITLED
Halifax Haunts: Exploring the City's Spookiest Spaces in an attempt
to create a do-it-yourself ghost tour of the city of Halifax. Now,
when a person sits down and writes a book, they are generally
trying to scratch a certain kind of itch. And writing *Halifax Haunts*
scratched that itch nicely—but I kept wondering to myself: what if
I could scratch just a little bit harder?

Well, time passed and I forgot that itch and wrote another
book instead, but then just this last summer, Nimbus contacted me
and asked me if I could write something along the lines of *Halifax
Haunts*—except instead of just writing a do-it-yourself ghost tour
of a single city, why not sit down and write a tour of the whole
danged province.

Sounds easy, doesn't it?

I mean, at 55,284 square kilometres, Nova Scotia is the
second-smallest province in the whole entire country. I mean, the
only province smaller than Nova Scotia is Prince Edward Island.

Still, there are an awful lot of ghost stories crammed inside our feisty little province. And I didn't want to *just* talk about ghost stories, you understand. I wanted to mention all of the weird and cool and interesting places to visit and think about in Nova Scotia—which covers a whole lot of territory, even in the second-smallest province in Canada. To make matters worse, I have already written about a lot of these haunted places. Still, there is just no way to write a guidebook to the haunted places in Nova Scotia *without* mentioning Sable Island, Devils Island, and Sacrifice Island.

Hmm…I wonder why so many of these ghosts seem to live on islands.

So anyway, I sat down and I came up with a total of fifty haunted and/or weird locations, with at least one story to go with each. And if you're so inclined, I've included the GPS coordinates to each spooky site, in case you want to experience it for yourself. But don't say I didn't warn you.

So now that I have the introduction out of the way, why don't you climb right in and get to reading some of these stories?

Yours in storytelling,
Steve Vernon

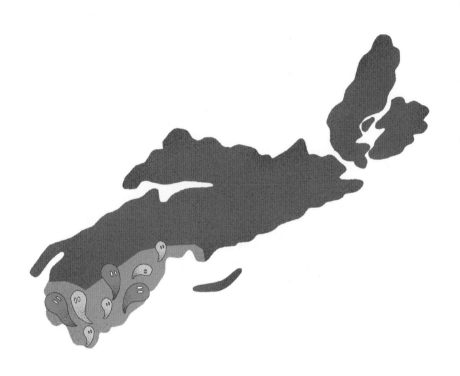

SECTION I
South Shore

1: The Ghosts of White Point Beach Resort

43.9659° N, 64.7358° W

ONE OF THE TRUE PLEASURES of my storytelling profession is when I am asked to go and tell stories in other parts of the province and/or the country. I have told my ghost stories several times down at the wonderful White Point Beach Resort and Lodge and I always have had a wonderful time there.

Originally founded in 1928 as a private hunting and fishing lodge, White Point eventually grew to become one of Nova Scotia's most well known vacation spots, employing almost two hundred Nova Scotia workers. Then, on November 12, 2011, tragedy struck: the main lodge caught fire and burned down.

Thanks to a lot of hard work, White Point Lodge was rebuilt and reopened exactly one year later, better than ever. Now, a lot of you folks might know that White Point Lodge is actually supposed to be haunted by not just one, but several ghosts.

Let me tell you a bit about them.

The most well known White Point ghost would be the spirit of Ivy. Ivy was the wife of Harvey Elliot, one of the earlier owners of the lodge. Ivy managed the resort's food and beverage department. She was, by all reports, a very tough lady to work for. She was a stickler for detail and would not put up with the slightest infraction of culinary etiquette. For example, if a piece of silverware was placed in the wrong location upon the dining tables Ivy would be known to pick up the offending bit of cutlery and fling it at whichever employee had the misfortune to misplace it.

To this day employees all have their own particular Ivy story, even though the woman passed away over fifty years ago.

"I was working late one evening about ten years back, setting the dining room for a large convention banquet that was scheduled to take place the very next day," Sid, a bartender at the Lodge's bar told me back in 2010, during my first Halloween visit to the lodge. "I was tired and I guess I had somehow misplaced a dessert spoon," Sid said. "By the time I realized my mistake I was absolutely exhausted. I did not want to go back and reset each of the tables for the sake of that one stupid spoon.

"At that point," Sid went on, "the dining-room lights went out. I fumbled in the dark for five whole minutes before finally finding the proper switch. When the lights came back on, I was surprised to see a dessert spoon flying at me, clanging off of my forehead and leaving a mark. I was even more surprised when I realized the entire dining room had been reset, with the dessert spoons all carefully re-laid in the proper position."

He grinned at this point and tipped me a wry wink.

"I don't really know if there is such a thing as ghosts," Sid said, "but I believe deep down in my heart of hearts that Ivy was looking out for me that night. She reset the tables and then she flung that spoon just to remind me not to make that same mistake twice. And do you know what?" Sid went on, "I haven't made that same mistake ever again. I just look at a dessert spoon and my head starts to ache all over again."

The interesting part of this story is that I heard similar tales from several of the wait staff as well as the people at the front desk. Ivy is still well known to the employees of the White Point Resort Lodge—but she isn't the only ghost that haunts this establishment.

There is also a ghost of a caretaker named Danny who resided in what was then known as Cabin 20, but is now Unit 137. Danny was a close friend of Ivy's and after she passed away he was often seen walking through the trails, talking to himself as if he were talking to his good friend Ivy.

The ghost of that old caretaker is still seen in front of his cabin. Sometimes he sits in a rocking chair while other times he is seen raking leaves in the autumn. Whenever anyone tries to get closer to the ghost he simply fades away or else steps behind a nearby tree and disappears.

Besides the ghost of Danny there is also a third ghost that haunts White Point Lodge. This would be the ghost of a nine-year-old boy whose family lived in the area in the early 1920s—back before the lodge was even built. The boy reportedly drowned while rafting off of White Point and his body was never recovered.

One look at the waves that relentlessly pound the White Point shoreline and you can imagine just how much difficulty a nine-year-old boy would have trying to steer a raft. Apparently, he had originally just set out to go a little ways into the water, but a rogue current caught the raft and led to his untimely demise.

The boy's ghost is the shyest spirit to haunt the lodge. His apparition is rarely seen, but he is always described as wearing old-fashioned overalls and a rumpled white shirt. He is most often spotted upon the rocks or else out on his raft, drifting eternally.

These three ghosts, in my opinion, definitely rank White Point Lodge a spot on my top ten-list of most haunted locations in Nova Scotia.

2: The Yarmouth County Jail

43.8375° N, 66.1174° W

CONSTRUCTED IN THE YEAR 1865, the brick-and-granite structure of the Yarmouth County Jail looms prominently over the smaller residential houses of Main Street, situated directly across from the Yarmouth Firefighters Museum.

The building contained living quarters for the jailer as well as his family. There were a total of nineteen jail cells as well as one large barred room that was used as a makeshift debtor's prison, for folks who could not pay their bills on time. The cells were laid out in tiers, with the bottom level being reserved for the male prisoners. The female and male prisoners who had yet to go to trial were kept on the upper floor.

The walls and ceiling were made out of concrete that was whitewashed yearly, as if to mask the despair, hatred, and guilt that lingered. Each cell was furnished with a sturdy iron bed frame that was fixed to the wall, topped with a straw mattress, two blankets, and no sheets or pillows.

There was a prison yard surrounded by a high fence, and the prisoners spent their time breaking rocks down into gravel for the streets of the town. Yup, sounds like it was a really great place to live, so long as you didn't have to stay there for more than a half an hour or so.

Over the years there have been many signs of hauntings within the cold, hard walls of the Yarmouth County Jail. Aside from the wildly varying temperature, water faucets turning on and off by themselves, and the sounds of moaning, shrieks, and hammering at nighttime, the eerie figure of a woman has been spotted wandering the corridors. She carries a lantern and appears to be looking for someone. Some witnesses of this phantom have also reported hearing the unmistakable footsteps of someone clicking along the wooden floorboards in a pair of fancy high-heeled shoes.

Darker still is the report of witnesses who swear they have heard the sound of a man screaming in the darkness, accompanied by the apparent reek of burning flesh. Experts believe this might be the ghost of Omar P. Roberts, who was convicted in a trial at the Yarmouth Courthouse in 1922 after burning his housekeeper, Flora Grey, to death in a fit of jealous rage. Roberts was madly obsessed with her and when she spurned his romantic advances due to his much greater age, hatred kindled deep within his heart. In his mindless anger he burned his house to the ground with Flora inside and got himself badly burned in the process.

Flora survived just long enough to identify Roberts as her murderer.

Omar P. Roberts was the last man to be hanged in Yarmouth. They hanged him at dawn on November 24, 1922. The execution was kept secret, for fear of a public uproar. The only witnesses reported were two local clergymen, the town doctor, the jailer, and a fellow prisoner who had been asked to assist in the duty. Roberts was also buried in secrecy. Most folks agree he was buried in an unmarked grave in the Yarmouth Cemetery; other folks have whispered that Omar P. Roberts was actually buried in behind the prison, in a quiet corner of the exercise yard.

It is his ghost people believe most frequently haunts the deserted halls of the Yarmouth County Jail. Interestingly, although the jailhouse served the Yarmouth region for almost 140 years, closing down in 2004, a local developer has purchased the old Yarmouth Jail from the township and intends to completely renovate the facility to construct a social and artistic hub. She hopes the darker history of the jailhouse will draw hordes of tourists.

"When we were kids we used to actually cross to the other side of the street rather than walk in front of the jail," the developer confessed. "With a little luck and a whole lot of work we might eventually manage to draw the kind of tourist traffic San Francisco enjoys with Alcatraz Island."

At the time of writing, the jailhouse is still in dire need of renovation. There is lead paint upon the walls. The building has no lighting, no working electrical system, and the plumbing is shot. The roof is nothing more than a thin funereal veil. It will take an awful lot of work to bring this old building back from the dead, but the developer hopes to eventually open up a full-scale restaurant on the top floor, a community performing art space on the second floor, and a small business centre in the basement.

I will be very interested to see what the ghosts make out of all of these brand new developments.

3: I Seen What I Says That I Seen

43° 29′ 39″ N, 65° 43′ 5″ W

AROUND 11:45 P.M. ON OCTOBER 4, 1967, a car full of Nova Scotian citizens witnessed a low-flying, brightly lit object careening into the cold starlit waters of Shag Harbour. An eighteen-year-old fisherman named Laurie Wickens was driving the car. Travelling along with Laurie was a long-time buddy of his, as well as their girlfriends. The four of them were returning home from a dance at Cape Sable Island, about thirteen miles to the east. It was a moonless night. The skies were calm and clear.

Almost ominous, some folks would say.

"We looked off to our right from the car and saw a line of lights flashing in the sky over the harbour," Laurie Wickens reported. "One would be on, and then another one and then a third and fourth in a kind of running sequence and then they'd all be on at once and then it'd start all over."

They thought the lights came from an airplane but it didn't

look like any airplane they had ever seen before. The lights steadily picked up speed, heading westward towards Shag Harbour.

"If it was a plane it was in trouble," Laurie Wickens went on. "It tipped this way and that way and then went down over a hill and we lost sight of it. By the time we crossed over the hill to where we could see it again, it had gone down into the water."

By the time they reached the waterfront several members of the town arrived to witness this eerie mystery soaring high above the waters of Shag Harbour. A pale-yellow, moon-shaped light hovered eight feet above the water and eight hundred feet from the shore, following the ebbing October tide and trailing a long wake of pale-yellow foam behind it.

"The foam stuff looked like a big floating giant snail trail," one witness said.

Laurie Wickens and his friends jumped back into their car and drove a half a mile further down the highway to a Lower Woods Harbour gas station. They fed a dime into a payphone and called the local RCMP detachment. Laurie Wickens reached RCMP Corporal Victor Werbicki at the Barrington detachment and reported what they'd seen.

"How much rum do you have in you, Laurie?" Corporal Werbicki asked. "One bottle or two?"

"Listen here, mister man, I'm as a sober as a Baptist judge on a Sunday morning," Laurie Wickens tartly replied. "And I seen what I says that I seen."

"My other desk phone is ringing," Werbicki said. "Just stay put and I'll send someone out there to see."

Werbicki hung up the phone. It rang again. Three more people phoned in reports of the eerie lights in the sky, and how they believed some sort of an aircraft had crashed into the cold depths of Shag Harbour.

This wasn't a joke.

Corporal Werbicki radioed two other constables on patrol, Ron O'Brian and Ron Pond, and the three Mounties drove down to the harbour.

Corporal Werbicki first reached local fisherman Lawrence Smith as he was heading for bed after a long day spent working on his boat.

"There's a plane down in the harbour," Werbicki told Smith. "I want you to go on out and have a look and see for us. I'm phoning Bradford Shand to bring his boat out as well."

"Makes sense to me," Smith replied. "Two boats can search better than one."

The two skippers and their crews took their boats out into the water searching for a crash site and possible survivors. The men were scared stiff of what they might find but they were determined to do their best to help out; yet all they discovered was that strange foamy slick, nearly eighty feet wide and a half a mile long swathing across the water of the Shag Harbour Sound.

"I wasn't too fussy about sailing into that foamy stuff," Lawrence Smith said. "But I didn't have much all that much say in the matter. You just couldn't avoid it, you understand."

The foam had the consistency of shaving cream, only with a glittering gold sheen across the surface. They even tried to scoop the weird floating foam up but the stuff just ran between their fingers.

"All we found was a patch of yellowish-brown foam on the water," Laurie Smith stated. "The colour looked a lot like burnt pancakes to me, you know when they are good and brown."

"That foam smelled foul," Shand added. "Just like burnt sulphur. It was nothing like any pancakes I ever breakfasted on."

The RCMP contacted the Joint Rescue Coordination Centre in Halifax, which in turn contacted the Coast Guard. By this time several other fishermen had showed up in their own fishing boats. A Coast Guard cutter joined them in their search an hour or so later and then reported to the RCMP: "No aircraft—private, commercial, or military—had been reported missing anywhere along the eastern seaboard of Canada or the northern United States."

Teams of Navy and Coast Guard divers descended down into the depths of the harbour, however they didn't find a thing. A day and a half later, the Canadian Defence Department issued the following memo:

"A preliminary investigation has been carried out by the Rescue Coordination Centre in Halifax and it has been determined that this UFO sighting wasn't caused by a flare, float, aircraft or any known object."

Other Reported Sightings

Mind you, the UFO sightings weren't strictly limited to the Shag Harbour area. Air Canada Captain Pierre Charbounneau, flying from the Halifax Stanfield International Airport on Air Canada Flight 305, pointed out to co-pilot Bob Ralph that there was something strange going on to the left of the aircraft at about 7:15 P.M. on the evening of October 4, 1967. The captain noted in his flight report that the two men observed a string of bright lights and a brilliantly lit rectangular object.

Both pilot and co-pilot reported seeing some sort of silent explosion, as if something had hit the aircraft. The two men agreed that it looked as if the whole thing faded into a blue hazy cloud.

At almost the very same time, author and Nova Scotia UFO expert Don Ledger reports in *The UFO Files* (Nimbus Publishing, 2007), that local Darrel Dorey, his sister Annette, and his mother were sitting on their front porch in Mahone Bay, when they noticed a large bright object manoeuvring above the southwestern horizon.

They weren't the only ones who saw something. UFO sightings were reported that day and the following from as far up the coast as Halifax Harbour. Now, while some of those sightings were undoubtedly just an easily explained outbreak of mass hysteria mixed with a dose of UFO fever, others were not as easily dismissed.

One Possible Theory

I recently read an editorial in the opinion pages of an October 2017 Halifax *Chronicle Herald* newspaper that suggested several unnamed fishermen owned a case of emergency flares, a few months too far beyond their "best before" date.

Fearing a possible mishap due to the flare's instability, the fishermen decided to set them off out at sea where they could do no damage. Following their impromptu fireworks display, the fishermen sailed back to Shag Harbour. When they spotted the RCMP and the crowd of people gathered at the shoreline they decided to opt for discretion—for fear that their harmless disposal of the bright rescue flares might get them into serious trouble.

So the unnamed fishermen discreetly mingled with the crowd and the fishing boats that were already investigating the situation and kept quiet about the whole thing. One never knows what is true or what is not in a situation like this. The Shag Harbour UFO incident has grown to near-mythic proportions. The little South Shore village has become known as Canada's very own Roswell— referring to the 1947 New Mexico incident that was either the crash of a weather balloon or the landing of an unreported flying saucer.

Like the fellow from *X-Files* says: "I want to believe."

How about you?

4: The Haunted Churchill Mansion
43.958125 N 66.133822 W

THE FUNNY THING ABOUT THE Churchill Mansion is that most ghost story collectors will tell you the mansion is located in Yarmouth. But actually, the mansion is located about eighteen kilometres north of Yarmouth, hidden along the Evangeline Trail, just outside of the small Acadian town of Port Maitland.

Aaron Flint Churchill, who was born in 1850 in the tiny village of Brooklyn, Nova Scotia, built the mansion. By his sixteenth year Flint stood six feet tall with an impressive set of ropy, work-hardened muscles, and he had made himself quite a reputation as a bold seafaring man aboard his uncle's ship, the *Research*.

Flint was serving as the first mate at the time of the voyage, November 10, 1866. Sixteen was young to be a first mate, but Flint had earned it honestly. He proved that after the ship's rudder snapped in two. Young Flint put together a makeshift rudder and clambered over the side into ice-cold water. After an hour and a half of struggling with ropes to secure the makeshift rudder, he was hauled back up to lay upon the deck and gather his strength.

A day later the second rudder snapped. Flint went over the side with a third jury-rigged rudder. In took eight rudders to complete the journey. Young Flint went into that water seven times in all. As a reward he was given a solid silver sextant and a chronometer watch as well as a two-thousand-dollar reward— which was a lot of money back in 1866.

Five years later he was given his own captaincy and four years after that he retired from his seafaring life at the age of twenty-four. He travelled to Savannah, Georgia, and he built a stevedoring business on the Savannah docks. Four years later he used his stevedore profits to start the Churchill Steamship Line. Shortly after, he bought a cotton plantation. His business ventures were highly profitable and he did well for himself.

In 1874, following his retirement, Aaron Flint Churchill decided to marry his second cousin, Lois Churchill, the daughter of William and Sarah Churchill, who resided in Yarmouth County. About ten years later, when a local doctor told the couple they couldn't have children of their own, Aaron and Lois made the best of it and adopted Aaron's niece Lotta May Churchill.

Lotta Churchill was born on May 13, 1885. She was the daughter of Aaron's brother George, who already had ten children of his own. Since Lotta was actually George's eleventh child, he saw no reason not to allow his brother and wife to adopt her.

Aaron Flint Churchill's business ventures continued to flourish and by the late 1800s he had become known as "the richest Canadian in America." In 1890 Flint had Churchill Mansion fully built and ready to move into. It took almost seven years to build the mansion, and Aaron decided to name the structure "The Anchorage."

"Here is where I'll drop my anchor," he said. "By the fresh calm water with the sun shining on the hillside and from here on out I'll enjoy country living and a nice cool breeze."

The Churchill Mansion loomed ominously over the quiet and still blue waters of Darlings Lake, which was named after Colonel Michael Ashley Darling. He was an officer from the garrison at Annapolis Royal, who had journeyed to Yarmouth for a surprise inspection of the local militia. He was so struck by the calm beauty of Darlings Lake that he decided to name it after himself.

The Mansion was huge, but oddly enough the Churchill family considered it their summer home. Their home in Savannah, Georgia, was even larger and more ostentatious. The Churchills enjoyed their luxury and weren't afraid to show off their wealth. Every spring the family arrived in Yarmouth on their very own steamship. All of their belongings were loaded onto wagons and pulled, caravan style, to their Darlings Lake mansion.

"It was like a great big old parade," one spectator reported in his diary. "There was nearly a mile of wagons and horses, stretched out and rolling straight on up Main Street all the way to Darlings Lake."

Following a two-year battle with illness, Aaron Flint Churchill passed away in Savannah, Georgia, on June 10, 1920. He was seventy years old, which was a good long life back then. His body was shipped back home, where he was buried in the family lot at Darlings Lake Cemetery.

Lois Churchill passed away almost seven years after her husband had died, on May 24, 1927. She was buried alongside him. As for Lotta, she travelled to Savannah and married a man by the name of Armand Rainey. She lived until May 24, 1971. Much has been made of the apparent fact that she had spent the last four years of her life in a sanatorium. Some paranormal investigators and storytellers hint that she was driven mad by a guilty past, however given that she was eighty-six when she died it is quite possible she was simply suffering from dementia.

Still, there are an awful lot of stories concerning Churchill Mansion.

The Ghosts of Churchill Mansion

Churchill Mansion has been visited many times over the years by several teams of practising ghost hunters.

In 2004 the Cold Spot Paranormal Research team—one of Canada's oldest paranormal investigation groups—became the first to visit. During their stay they experienced several unexplainable temperature shifts as well as isolated cold spots. Loud thumping footsteps were heard, and one of the investigators said he felt an invisible hand reach in through his chest and squeeze his lung.

In 2006 the colourful and slightly outlandish Rescue Mediums paid a visit to the mansion for the thirteenth episode of their reality show's first season. They spoke of sensing a ghostly apparition of a woman in white walking down the road towards the mansion. Locals have often reported seeing this particular apparition. Sometimes she is seen walking from the graveyard while other times she walks right out of the depths of Darlings Lake and up the hill towards Churchill Mansion. Some folks believe, due to the apparition's lonely sad eyes, that the Woman in White might actually be the spirit of Lotta herself, still haunting this location.

The Rescue Mediums also got a very bad feeling from a portrait of Aaron Flint Churchill, and they agreed that the spirit of Lotta was indeed haunting the building that she had grown up in. The Rescue Mediums claim to have successfully exorcised Lotta's dead spirit and sent her on her way to the other side; however, in 2008 local paranormal investigator Paul Andrew Kimball paid a visit to the Churchill mansion and reported strange chills and doors that opened and closed of their own accord.

Paul Kimball spoke with the current owner of the building, Bob Benson, who told Paul that whenever the portrait of Lotta was removed from its usual position on the wall, bad luck immediately followed. Paul concluded his investigations by reporting that although nothing specifically supernatural had occurred, his crew had witnessed enough unexplained activity that he felt that the mansion was still very much haunted by the ghost of Lotta May Churchill.

In early 2009 the Churchill Mansion property was purchased for approximately $300,000 by a British Columbia entrepreneurial couple who had intended to turn it into an up-to-date bed and breakfast. In the spring of 2013 the bed and breakfast began taking in guests again.

Interestingly enough, I have not come across any recent reports of anomalous ghostly activity at the Churchill Mansion—however, this prominent Darlings Lake edifice is still regularly reported as being one of Nova Scotia's most haunted locations.

Why don't you book a visit and make up your mind for yourself?

5: The Frost Park Phantom

43.8375° N, 66.1174° W

LET ME TELL YOU ABOUT a charming little oasis that used to be a graveyard. It is known as Frost Park, located on Main Street in Yarmouth, directly across the street from the Izaak Walton Killam Memorial Library, where my mother, Madge, worked for many years. She often used to sit in the park smoking one of her long cigarettes and reading one of the many books from the library.

Frost Park is a lovely spot for relaxing and daydreaming, but as I mentioned, up until 1860, early settlers used it as a burial ground.

And why not? It was a picturesque location, it was handy to walk to, and the ground was soft for the digging. In 1861 Yarmouth Mountain Cemetery was built as a replacement burial ground. Some of the previously buried bodies were moved from Frost Park to the Yarmouth Mountain Cemetery, approximately two kilometres away, but there are other folks who still rest here, their graves still marked by their tombstones.

It is an interesting juxtaposition: the rest of the gravesite existing side-by-side a spot for simple leisure activities. There is a beautiful fountain and a look-off point that looks out across the downtown waterfront. There are fine benches to sit upon and curved stone walls that offer surprisingly wonderful acoustics. Just try it yourself, if you don't believe me. Stand in the middle of the park and speak in a normal voice and your friends—who you have hopefully instructed to stand by the curved walls—will hear you as if you are standing right beside them.

Further down in the park you will find a memorial to the folks who have been lost at sea in the Yarmouth region. There are sculptures and a gazebo and beds of flowers of many different varieties as well, but if you really want to see this park in all its beauty and splendour swing down in the winter when the trees in the park are festooned with decorative lights. It is breathtakingly awe-inspiring.

Oh, and there is a ghost as well.

The Frost Park Phantom

Let me tell you about that ghost. First off, there might be more than one ghost. Remember, there are still graves here in the park, and even not counting the graves that are marked there have been many more burials that were not recorded. Funerals used to be a whole lot more casual affairs than they are in modern days. Back then there was a little less sentiment and a lot more practicality. Basically, the way that our ancestors saw it was that they were dead and they had to be put somewhere.

Why not put them in the ground?

Anyway, in the early 1970s a fellow by the name of Ralph Surette claimed to have seen and spoken to the Frost Park Phantom many times.

"He is always wearing a long brown jacket and a tall felt hat and he smoked one of those big-hooked calabash pipes, the kind that look like something you might have stolen them from Sherlock Holmes," Surette said. "I used to see the ghost down in

Frost Park, walking with the aid of a long wooden cane."

Surette went on to tell of how the ghost gave him directions to a vast treasure of at least a million dollars on Eastern Bar Island, located in the Eastern Channel of the Tusket River.

"Only I never could find that treasure," Surette said. "No matter how hard I looked."

Treasure or not, the Frost Park Phantom has been spotted by a lot more than just one witness. Tourists and locals have seen the old man many times throughout the years. He always is walking slowly and quietly and he never seems to be interested in stirring up any sort of trouble.

The next time you are down in Yarmouth make sure that you take a walk through Frost Park and see if you can see him. Maybe he will even give you a tip on how to find that missing treasure.

6: The Heartsick Ghost of Seal Island
43° 24' 47" N, 66° 0' 42" W

SEAL ISLAND LIES ABOUT TWENTY-SEVEN kilometres northeast of Shag Harbour. Samuel de Champlain discovered it in 1604, and named it *Île aux loups-martins* after the seals—or "sea-wolves" as they were called then—colonizing the island's coast. Actually, Champlain named the whole cluster of islands the Seal Islands, but nowadays there is just the one island locals refer to as Seal Island.

This isn't an easy place to visit. There isn't a ferry or regular boat service to Seal Island. The crossing takes about two hours of hard sailing and you need to be ready to row yourself ashore. It is a small island, about four square kilometres in total, and it is surrounded on its east, south, and west sides by a series of dangerous rocky shoals.

These days most folks make it a point to stay away from Seal Island. Not because of the danger, mind you; most folks stay away from Seal Island because it is haunted by the ghost of Annie Lindsay.

The Lonely Love of Annie Lindsay

Stories, like sea-borne storms, can start an awful long way from where they wind up getting to. A tiny miller moth flaps its dusty wings a thousand miles and somewhere out to sea the wind stirs up and a storm is born.

Annie's story begins on the Blonde Rock, a ridge of shoals nine kilometres south-southeast of Seal Island. The shoal isn't named for the colour of the rocks or the colour of any particular person who drowned next to those rocks. Rather, the shoal cluster was named after the frigate HMS *Blonde*, a prison ship that was wrecked upon this fateful rock way back in 1782. Barely sixty men survived the wreck.

Over a hundred years later the SS *Ottawa*, a brand-new, 27,600-ton, solid-steel steamer, steamed straight into the mouth of a roaring gale and broke itself wide open upon the tooth of the Blonde Rock.

It was Halloween night when the gale first hit, a Saturday in 1891. The SS *Ottawa* struck the Blonde Rock at 5 A.M. Sunday. The rock stove a large hole into the hull of the vessel and the steamer filled with seawater as the tide came in.

The lifeboats were launched.

Four sailors as well as a stewardess by the name of Annie Lindsay, the only lady on-board, got onto the lifeboat and rowed just as hard as they could for the shores of Seal Island. Annie was a quiet, plain-looking girl. The sailors said she was hard working and serious. What they didn't know was Annie had a secret.

She loved one of the sailors. She didn't possess the boldness of spirit to tell this man of the feelings she had buried deep within her. She looked at him when he worked but if he felt her gaze she turned her head and looked out towards the calling sea.

She was just too scared to tell him what she felt.

Every morning she awoke and told herself she would speak

her heart to this man but every evening she went to sleep holding the unspoken words still within her. It was hard to tell someone that sort of a feeling when you worked with them as Annie did. She feared the possibility of fights and jealousy and the possible loss of her job. She feared his rejection even more.

And then the storm hit and the ship had broken upon the Blonde Rock and the men had fled for the dubious safety of the lifeboat.

Rowing a boat in a heavy sea is not as easy as you might think. An hour passed and the crew had managed to row about two ship length's work of distance—maybe 170 metres away from the sinking vessel—when a huge wave broke over the lifeboat and turned it completely over. Two of the sailors managed to clamber up onto the bottom of the lifeboat and then, after much effort, they dragged two other sailors up from the water. The two men dragged out of the water were half-frozen to death and the other two were in hardly any better condition. The four of them hung on grimly to the overturned keel of the lifeboat and eventually drifted ashore on Seal Island.

The lifeless form of Annie Lindsay washed ashore the very next morning. She was the only casualty and the crew mourned her passing deeply.

"You loved her, didn't you?" one sailor asked the other.

"No," the other sailor replied. "I never said a thing to her at all. I thought it was you who loved her and I did not want to stand in your way."

I guess sometimes even love needs a road map.

There were no relatives or kinfolk of Annie Lindsay to be found, so the lighthouse keeper took it upon himself to dig Annie a grave beside the walls of the Seal Island Church and then he carved a wooden tombstone in honour of her constant memory. That tombstone is still there and folks will not move it.

It is said that the ghost of Annie Lindsay still walks these shores on long and lonely October nights when the island is empty of life and the wind blows loudly and the storms run high. Some folks believe that her spirit is trying to get back to her family, wherever they might be. However, some believe that her body was exhumed many years after her death and there were signs that she had been buried alive. There were claw marks on the inside of the homemade casket and the corpse's fingernails were broken down—and it is for this reason that her ghost still haunts this island.

7: The Yarmouth Runic Stone

43°50'12.25"N 66°06'56.6"W

IN THE YEAR 1812, NOTED Yarmouth physician Dr. Richard Fletcher made a startling discovery. Not far from the Overton Salt Pond Dam (also known as the Chegoggin Flats), in the salt marsh, he found a four-hundred-pound stone covered in fourteen mysterious rune-like markings.

Fletcher had been an army surgeon, born in 1749 and educated in medicine at the University of Aberdeen, and had served in the fever-ridden regions of the West Indies. Although Dr. Fletcher died in March 1818, the runic stone remained on display at his property for sixty years until it was moved into Yarmouth proper.

The stone was nothing fancy, just common quartzite, or what was more often known back then as county stone, a popular choice for wall or fence building. The stone had been split off from a larger chunk of rock. It must have taken Dr. Fletcher, who would have been about sixty-three years old at the time, an awful lot of effort to hew and move the runic stone. Still, with six children to his name, he might have had some help moving the artefact.

The so-called runes that are engraved upon the stone have conjured up an awful lot of interesting theories as to their exact origin. They have been studied by numerous experts who claim that the runes are actually Viking, Chinese, Semitic, Siberian, Hebrew, early Greek, or even Spanish. I guess that it is pretty hard to run a successful DNA test on a four-hundred-pound rock.

The stone is alternately referred to as either the Yarmouth Runic Stone or the Mystery Stone, or the Fletcher Stone. A short time after the stone had been transported from its resting place on Dr. Fletcher's front lawn, the provincial inspector of mines arranged to have the Yarmouth Mystery Stone moved to the Provincial Museum in Halifax. However, a glitch in paperwork prevented that from ever happening.

Shortly before the outbreak of the First World War the stone was transported to Kristiania, Norway (now known as Oslo), where it was proudly displayed at an international exhibition. It was then stored in the London offices of the Canadian Pacific Railway for safekeeping during the war. It was just too dangerous to risk losing the runic stone to a lucky shot from a German U-boat. Following the Armistice of 1918 the stone was finally returned to its original home in Yarmouth.

For a time it fell into the hands of a private owner who arranged to have it placed in front of the Yarmouth Public Library. Following a bit of legal and political decision-making the artifact was given over to the care of the Yarmouth County Historical Society and the runic stone was moved inside to the Yarmouth County Museum where you can see it today.

More Stones Than You Can Throw a Rock At

Mind you, the Fletcher Runic Stone wasn't the only mysterious geological artefact to be unearthed in the Yarmouth area.

In the year of 1897 a second stone was discovered at the Bay View Park, a tourist resort directly across the harbour from the town of Yarmouth, just about a single kilometre from the original location of the Fletcher Stone. The stone was found, face downward and half-buried in the mud by James F. Jeffrey, who had been constructing a stone wall and had simply seen it as a handy piece of stone.

The Bay View Park stone looked an awful lot like the Fletcher Stone, except with a few more mysterious rune-like markings on a second line below the first. Unfortunately, the Bay View Park stone was carelessly picked up by a work crew who thought it would fit perfectly in a new stone wall that they were building, on the former Burrill property in Yarmouth, just handy to the southeast corner of Starrs Road and Pleasant Street.

Prior to that, in February 1880, a letter from Doctor T. B. Flint (and would you *really* want to go and see a doctor whose first two initials were T. B.?) stated he had discovered two very large stones on a small island near the mouth of the Tusket River, with inscriptions similar to the Fletcher Stone.

"The spot was very difficult to access by land, but not by water, although it is not in any regularly frequented route," Flint wrote.

Unfortunately, he never revealed the exact location of these two very large stones. You might want to go looking yourself sometime but do not expect to see me out there hunting for a new Nova Scotia answer to Stonehenge. I generally do my best to avoid the dreaded Nova Scotia mosquito and there is an abundance of them out in the Yarmouth woods.

8: Where The Blue Lady Walks

44° 29′ 34″ N, 63° 55′ 3″ W

TOURISM CANADA PROUDLY BRAGS THAT out of the over 160 historic lighthouses still standing along the shores of Nova Scotia, no other lighthouse has been photographed, painted, or YouTubed more than the picturesque lighthouse standing proudly on the shores of Peggys Cove.

Now, what an awful lot of people do not realize is that Peggys Cove is actually haunted by a lonely blue ghost.

The way folks tell the story around Peggys Cove is that Peggy was the name of a woman who had been washed ashore after a shipwreck out in the waters of the St. Margaret's Bay. Well, actually she could not remember her real name. All that she could remember was that she had lost her family out there in the ocean when the ship that she had been travelling on had gone down, or possibly that she had left her family back in Europe. That is how some people deal with pain that is just too great for their heart to bear. They dig a hole in their banks of their memory and they bury it away. The story was awfully muddy and blurred. Either way, she could not remember her name or at least she claimed not too, so the townsfolk decided to name her Peggy (a common nickname for Margaret), after St. Margaret's Bay.

A young fisherman by the name of Angus was struck by Peggy's beauty and began to court her, determined to make her his wife.

"You need to cheer up," he would tell her. "You have lost your old life but there is no reason why you cannot start a whole brand new life all over again with me. Leave your tears to sink into the ocean. That is what salt water is for."

Apparently, when Peggy still bleakly refused to smile at Angus's efforts to cheer her up, he decided to clown around a bit and see if he could make her laugh. After all, laughter was the very best medicine there was, or at least that was how Angus saw it.

So Angus climbed up onto that heap of rocks where the famous Peggys Cove Lighthouse stands and he attempted to perform an Irish jig, a tricky-enough step upon solid ground, let alone upon the slippery wet rocks of Peggys Cove.

Angus lost his footing and he fell to the rock and broke his skull open and before Peggy knew it the poor man had died. Peggy's heart had been broken again, even before she had allowed it to heal from her first great loss.

She turned her back upon Angus's cold body, walked slowly down to the black rocks, stepped into the very first crashing wave, and drowned herself. To this day, people swear that they see her ghost still walking the rocks of Peggys Cove, still dressed in that cornflower-blue smock she always wore.

Some people see her standing upon the black rocks—meaning the rocks that are close enough to the sea's edge to be splashed by the waves. Most locals know to steer clear of these so-called black rocks, although at least once a year you will read about some poor misguided soul who fell in, and a few have even been washed out to sea. Even the rocks that aren't black are risky, because waves can surprise you as they rise up onto the higher rocks.

"The waves there almost seem to reach out and grab hold of you like they want to pull you in and drown you," one tourist told me. "You have got to be careful standing that close to the sea."

Some people believe that Peggy's ghost chooses to stand near those black rocks to warn the unwary tourists to beware of the slippery rocks. Other people believe in the shadows of the story. Their theory is that the ghost of Peggy still haunts these lonely rocks, hoping to lure unwary tourists down into the waters below. Perhaps she is looking for company in her lonely vigil.

Perhaps she is looking for vengeance against the fate that stole the lives of everyone she ever came to love and cherish.

I cannot tell you which of these theories are true. Still, I encourage you to make a visit to Peggys Cove the first chance you get and see if you can catch a glimpse of Peggy as she walks upon the shoreline. Maybe you ought to wave at her and see if you can get her to smile back at you.

Just make sure you pay close attention to those signs and stay away from the slippery black rocks. I don't care how cool a selfie you can get, no thrill on earth is worth drowning for.

SECTION 2
Western Shore

9: The Parker Road Phantom
45° 2′ 51.17″ N, 64° 44′ 9.42″ W

A LOT OF FOLKS IN THE Aylesford and Berwick area might have heard of this story. Actually, a good friend told me she remembered the whole thing from back when she was growing up in the Berwick area—so let me throw out a quick wave to Shelley-who-knew, which is probably going to confuse the heck out of the three other Shelleys I happen to know.

Well, anyway, Shelley-who-knew read the short version of this tale that I had previously included in my children's picture book, *Maritime Monsters*.

"Hey," Shelley-who-knew said. "I remember that happening back when I was growing up. I didn't think anyone outside of Berwick knew that story."

After the picture book was published I got the chance to speak to noted cryptozoologist and Bigfoot historian, Loren Coleman (author of *Mysterious America, Cryptozoology: A to Z - The Encyclopedia Of Loch Monsters, Sasquatch, Chupacabra, and Other*

Authentic Mysteries of Nature) at the East Coast Paracon in 2016. He was also quite surprised to see that I knew the true story behind the Parker Road Phantom.

He knew the truth as well, being an expert in this field—but he pointed out that an awful lot of well-known and often-published cryptozoologists still reported the Parker Road Phantom as being a mystery that was yet to be solved—when the truth was a couple of locals had already confessed to the whole thing some time ago.

Mind you, I've never claimed to be much of a cryptozoologist or even a ghost hunter or anything like that at all. I am nothing more than an old-school storyteller. I belong behind a campfire, rather than a Ouija board, infrared/ultrasonic motion detector, or even behind a well-water-detecting willow-dowsing rod—which probably would give me a handful of slivers for my troubles if I ever really tried to use one.

No sir and no ma'am. I just sat down and I did my research and I talked to people and I did my very best to listen even more than I talked—which is how I found out that what had been reported to be a giant seventeen-to-eighteen foot tall supernatural phantom wasn't actually all that supernatural at all. It was actually the work of five bored young Berwick boys who decided to see if they could fool their grandparents.

Let me tell you how the story goes.

The whole thing all started out in the year 1969—while The Beatles were making their very last public appearance, and France was revving up their brand new supersonic Concorde Jet, and every young man of legal age was dreaming about owning a brand new racing-striped Pontiac Firebird Trans Am muscle car—when five young Berwick boys were sitting down together in their grandparents' barn, plotting a little simple happy foolishness.

"I'm bored," Billy Gates said.

"Me too," his brother Ronny said.

"I have gone way past being bored," David Gates added. "In fact I am pretty sure I am slowly slipping into a coma over here."

"Like anyone would ever notice if you did or not," Tommy

Gates, who was the biggest of the four brothers said. "The only time I have ever seen you wake up was when you needed to roll over and have yourself a nap."

"I thought I remembered dreaming that," David Gates said.

"Yeah," Billy said. "Right before the teacher woke you up."

Which wasn't really true but being brothers, like these four were, it was expected of them to sit around and trade insults with each other.

"I know what we can do," Dicky Taylor said.

Dicky Taylor was Tommy's best friend and could always be counted for on coming up with an idea—which he did—which was how the whole big plan first got started. One of the boys borrowed his grandfather's great big long old army war coat and an old watch cap that smelled just about as funky as a bucket full of sun-rotted sardines.

Little Billy got up on top of Tommy's shoulders with the old war coat hung over his shoulders and draped down over Tommy's head and shoulders, so anyone looking could not see Tommy beneath the coat.

Billy also wore one of his mother's nylon stockings pulled down over his face to help muddle his features and disguise him, just in case anyone actually got close enough to catch a look at the two boys.

Come the first foggy night, the two boys went out in their monster-coat costume. It hadn't really started as being a monster, mind you. They just figured they'd look like a big scary man and they did actually give their mother Violet Gates a pretty good scare when they looked straight in her kitchen window.

They decided to see if they could scare the cars rolling by on Parker Road—only when the first car drove by and the driver got a look at little Billy and Tommy in their disguise, he nearly drove his car off of the side of the road.

Faster than you could say "Loch Ness dog paddle," word got out that there was a gigantic creature prowling the side of Parker Road. Folks began to drive up and down the road with the idea of taking a shot at the monster—with either a Kodak camera or a Remington pump-action shotgun.

The boys had a plan, though. One of them sat up in the loft and kept watch for any cars that were getting too close. The boys had set up a base camp in the old barn and whenever they were spotted, Billy would jump off of Tommy's shoulders and the two of them would keep low and run for the barn. Two of the other kids stood ready and waiting by the barn doors and slammed the door shut.

Mind you, things almost went bad when a pair of hunters, who had driven all the way up from Morristown, kept their headlights turned off and sneaked into the barn and almost caught the boys by surprise. The boys ran for cover. One of them took shelter under an old beat-up green Coleman canoe stored down in the family root cellar.

Word spread across the country as articles turned up in Prairie newspapers and the *Toronto Star*. This was long before the internet had even been dreamed of, but the Parker Road Phantom *definitely* went viral. With every new story told about the Phantom, the legend took even wilder shape.

Some folks claimed the Phantom was seven feet tall. Others grew him up to twelve feet and one article described him as twenty feet tall. He was said to leap buildings like Superman and that he often issued blood-curdling screams capable of turning a young man's hair grey. One author even reported the Parker Road Phantom as having giant green feet—although Tommy later told reporters he preferred a pair of white Converse sneakers.

There was a boost in Berwick's tourism and the local restaurant really appreciated the extra business; however, not everyone was all that pleased about the situation. All of the kids and the teachers as well in the local schoolhouse talked about the Phantom and people began to worry that the beast might someday decide to run amok.

Eventually the boys felt bad about the whole thing and decided to turn themselves in to the local police, who got a pretty good laugh out of the whole story. They didn't punish the boys. Instead, they built a great big parade float, which they put into the Berwick Gala Day Parade. Tommy and Billy rode on the top of that parade float dressed in their full Phantom gear, stinky watch cap and all.

To me, that is the coolest part of the whole story and it goes to show you just how powerful a muscle a child's imagination can be. Just think about how five young kids created a legend that lives on to this very day—almost fifty years later.

Who knows? Maybe someday you and a few of your best friends might build your own monster—only watch out for those Morristown shotguns.

10: **The Stem-ta-Stern Hanged Man**

*220 Granville Street, Annapolis County, Route 1,
along the Annapolis River*

ONE OF THE QUESTIONS PEOPLE sometimes ask me is if I know of a hotel they can stay in—only it needs to be actually haunted. I guess for some folks just reading about such events isn't enough. They need to *experience* the whole thing, which is why they come to me.

It's a tall order, but I do know of a couple of locations you might try. One such place is located in the small Nova Scotia community of Bridgetown, which is known by some folks to be "the prettiest little town in Nova Scotia." However, there is one aspect of this town that is not so pretty. It seems there is a persistent ghastly visitation of a hanged man who appears at the bedroom window outside of the Stem-ta-Stern Bed and Breakfast, a Queen Anne Revival House built way back in 1868.

Just try and picture that, now will you?

Imagine yourself fast asleep in your bed, when all of a sudden the temperature plummets as if you took a fast-freight elevator ride down into the frozen ninth circle of Dante's inferno. Then, as you shiver alone in the darkness, you hear a strange tapping at the window. So you rise up out of the bed and open the curtains and look outside to the see the rotted remains of a man hanging by his neck from a ratty old rope slung over the branches of a nearby tree, swaying patiently in the evening breeze. Imagine the bony right arm of that remnant of a man is sticking out stiffly in the twisted rigors of ancient death, with the sickly yellowed fingernails of a long bony hand tapping persistently at your window.

And he is staring at you.

This ghastly apparition has been witnessed many times over the years. Even after a change in ownership, the new owner reported that on two separate evenings she bore witness to the sight of that hideous dangling figure.

"On the very first week that I moved in I saw it at the window," she said. "I was terrified, but it did not seem to mean me any harm."

Then two weeks later the temperature in the bedroom dropped like a stone down a well, and the owner heard that same persistent scratching at the window again.

"I told myself the scratching was nothing but the rattle of the wind," she explained. "I told myself I didn't need to go to the window to look and see. I told myself it was nothing more than the wind moving a branch against the window pane."

Yet, when she opened up her eyes the figure was standing in the very bedroom itself, scowling right at her. His face was swollen blue and purple and his neck was rope burned and twisted into a nearly ninety-degree angle.

"I wanted to scream just as loudly as I could scream," she said. "But something told me that my screaming wouldn't do me any good. So instead I took a deep breath in and I forced myself to calmly speak."

And this is what she told that ghost: "I am sorry, but we are closed for the night. If you are looking for a room you will have to look elsewhere."

When I asked her if that trick worked for her, she just smiled and shrugged.

"He looked confused," she admitted, "as if he hadn't expected me to say that. I wasn't about to allow this spirit to ruin my evening. He slowly vanished, like an old-time photograph developing itself in reverse. Then, once he disappeared I felt certain that he was going to reappear again, so that evening I went to bed and pulled the blankets up over my head."

"And did you sleep?" I asked her.

"Not a wink," she confessed.

Are you still interested in booking a room at the Stem-ta-Stern Bed and Breakfast? And more importantly, are you brave enough to go and spend the night?

11: The Two Battles of Bloody Creek
44° 49′ 0″ N, 65° 17′ 0″ W

SLITHERING QUIETLY DOWN INTO THE rolling flow of the mighty Annapolis River, about two or three miles southeast of Bridgetown and very close to the little town of Carleton Corner, you will find the meandering length of Bloody Creek. This creek is famous in Nova Scotia history for having been the location of two separate battles. Oddly enough, both were known as the Battle of Bloody Creek.

Now this is a ghost-story guide rather than a history book, so I am going to go over the battles in a very abbreviated manner which ought to be easy, considering that both of them were fought over the very same reason—but there are ghost stories told about each of these battles.

The First Battle of Bloody Creek
The first battle occurred in 1710. A force of New England militiamen and British marines lead by Francis Nicholson captured

Port Royal from the French. They renamed the settlement Annapolis Royal and elected Samuel Vetch to serve as the British governor of Nova Scotia and likewise renamed the fort, Fort Anne.

The problem was the 450 men were not enough to defend the fort from the French forces. Worse yet, the British had a hard time keeping their troops supplied. The local Acadian population were responsible for all of the shipping and they weren't fond of the British.

"We can't work for you," the Acadians told the British. "You don't like us. You pay us in paper, rather than gold. You can't even protect us if we go out logging for you and the French troops and their Abenaki allies."

"Listen," the British commander said. "Just trust me."

Never trust anyone who asks you to trust them.

On June 10, 1711, a force of 70 British troops left Fort Anne, sailing up the Annapolis River in a whaling dory and two flatboats. Unfortunately for the British, the French and the Abenaki were ready for them. A party of at least 150 men, French and Abenaki alike, were waiting to ambush the British forces at the mouth of Bloody Creek. They caught the British in a perfect crossfire, setting the boats on fire and wiping out the British troops.

For years afterwards, that whaleboat has been seen sailing down the length of Bloody Creek while ghostly flames roar and crackle and dance about it. The ghosts of the British troops have often been seen upon that whaleboat, firing their guns into the air and howling like a pack of laryngitis-stricken wolves.

It is also rumoured the Acadians left behind a large chest of gold and jewels, sunken in the roiling depths of Bloody Creek. On moonlit nights you can still see the glitter of the gold coins glimmering in the strong rushing waters of Bloody Creek—but in case you get the idea of indulging in a little impromptu treasure hunting, I would recommend that you wait until the sun is high in the sky. You might not like what you find on the haunted creek around the cold and lonely hours past midnight.

The Second Battle of Bloody Creek

On December 8, 1757, a second major battle broke out upon this very site, only this time the conflict was waged between a detachment of 130 British troops from out of Annapolis Royal defending themselves against a combined group of Mi'kmaw and Acadian rebels.

I guess that the British *still* hadn't learned how to get along with either the Indigenous population or the Acadians. It might have been easier if the two nations had just thrown a big old potluck dinner and hashed their differences out over a few fast-paced rounds of cutthroat cribbage.

It didn't help that the British decided to make peace with the French Acadians by evicting them from the province. That's right, two years prior to the Second Battle of Bloody Creek, the British announced what they colourfully referred to as the Great Expulsion.

"You can go anywhere you want to," the British told the Acadians. "But you can't stay here."

Which is one way of dealing with your unwanted dinner guests, I guess.

The second battle went down much like the first. The British attempted to cross Bloody Creek and were greeted with a hail of gunfire, and in a very short time approximately fifty French troops, aided by some rebel Acadians and a group of Mi'kmaq, drove off over three hundred British soldiers and officers.

Between those two battles, it kind of makes you wonder just how the British ever managed to win out over the French here in Canada, now doesn't it?

The ghosts of those fallen British troops are said to still practice their drill formations, marching proudly, deep beneath the waters of Bloody Creek. On certain moonlit nights those same raging waters are said to run as red as freshly spilled blood.

Between the two battles and the two sets of ghost stories told around them, I would have to say that Bloody Creek ranks high on my list of most-haunted locations in Nova Scotia.

12: The Bloody Creek Crater
44°45′00″N 65°14′30″W

I DON'T KNOW ABOUT YOU, BUT I have had a secret
and slightly unsettling fear of falling objects. I suppose that
is understandable, since back in the days when I worked in a
warehouse I fell off a six-foot ladder, which broke beneath the
combined weight of myself and the boxed lawn mower I had been
attempting to set on a top shelf. It had been the boss's idea that I put
it up there and it had been the boss's budgetary restraints that had
us using household ladders as opposed to industry-grade ladders.

All the same, I kind of wonder if that boss ever really liked me.

I suppose that the fear of falling objects is really no great
mystery, but I am not talking about those kinds of falling objects. I
am talking about objects falling out of the clear blue nowhere sky.

Mind you, there are actual precedents for my secret worry.

In 1936 a meteorite struck a Newfoundland fishing boat and
apparently set it afire. The fire was put out and there were no
casualties but the crew all admitted that it was a pretty close

encounter—and that the worst of it was, it most likely scared the fish.

In 1954 a thirty-four-year-old woman by the name of Ann Hodges living in Sylacauga, Alabama, was smacked in her side by an eight-pound meteorite which smashed through her roof, ricocheted off her radio, and slammed into her thigh, leaving a pineapple-sized welt while she lay quietly sleeping upon her living-room couch.

No, I am *not* making that up.

Go ahead and Google it if you have to for further details, but while you are busy Googling I suggest you try thinking about that the next time you feel the urge to lie down and take a nap. Maybe you really don't need that sleep at all.

Let me give you another example.

On October 5, 1992, a meteor shard weighing approximately a pound and a half smashed directly through the trunk of a housewife's parked 1980 Chevy Malibu Classic in Peekskill, New York. Authorities first thought that the car had either been bombed or a piece of an aircraft had fallen upon it; however, subsequent studies proved that it was actually an honest-to-Superman meteorite. Since then the car has been displayed at trade shows and museums across the world including the New York City's American Museum of Natural History and France's National Museum of Natural History. That's not too shabby for a 1980 Chevy, eh?

How about this example?

Around midnight on March 26, 2003, a sustained flurry of hundreds of meteorites rained on the Chicago suburbs of Park Forest and Olympia Fields, about thirty-five miles southwest of downtown Chicago. The larger meteorites punched huge holes in house roofs and dented cars. One meteorite embedded itself in the Park Forest fire station.

So they are out there and they are falling out the sky—maybe not all of the time but enough to keep this old storyteller wondering and worrying.

Let's look at the numbers.

According to the laws of statistics, there is a 1-in-700,000 chance of being actually struck by lightning here in North America. Furthermore, lightning strikes killed over 4,000 people in the last fifty years.

So I wonder just what the odds are for being struck by a meteorite.

US astronomer Alan W. Harris has gone ahead and made that calculation. I'm not sure just *why* he ever bothered to figure it all out. I mean, maybe it was just a slow night on television. Still, allowing for the number of Earth-crossing asteroids—the kind that can hit us because their individual orbits around the Sun intersect ours—as well as how much damage they can do (which depends on their size), he calculated that any person's lifetime odds of being killed by an asteroid impact are about 1 in 700,000—exactly the same odds as someone being struck by lightning.

Now do not get me wrong. You will not find me walking around the house wearing a construction worker's hardhat, and my wife has made me throw away my tinfoil hat.

Still, just stop and think about it, would you? One out of 700,000 are pretty low odds for any sort of a statistic, and certainly not enough of a risk for me to lie awake at night worrying about it.

Now you might be wondering just what in the world a confession of out-of-the-clear-blue-sky-o-phobia might have to do with weird Nova Scotia places.

Well, let me tell you about Nova Scotia's most famous meteor crater.

The Bloody Creek Crater

The Bloody Creek Crater is a 420-by-350-metre meteor crater that was discovered back in 1987 by Dr. George R. Stevens, a retired geologist from Acadia University, located in nearby Wolfville. Unfortunately, for those folks out there who might actually want to have a look at the crater, it had been completely submerged a little less than ten years before, after Nova Scotia Power constructed a hydroelectric dam across a short stretch of Bloody Creek and created the provincial reservoir now known as Dalhousie Lake.

The crater is located between the town of Bridgetown and the community of West Dalhousie. It has been described as an elliptically shaped crater with a rim surrounding the entirety of it and standing about a metre high. Inside the crater is a mossy and almost swamp-like fen. It is one of only 127 recorded extraterrestrial impact craters, which is a really fancy of saying "this is right where the meteor hit." Crater experts refer to the Bloody Creek crater as the Astrid Crater.

Now, what I really want to know is just how a fellow goes about becoming a crater expert. I mean, what sort of a notion would have to strike you as a child to make you want to grow up and study holes in the ground anyway? Of course, I know a lot of people who feel the very same way about ghost-story collecting.

Sadly, the only way that you can actually see the crater these days is with the help of some good-quality scuba gear. The crater has surfaced a couple of times when Nova Scotia Power had to drain Dalhousie Lake in order to make repairs upon the hydroelectric works. Just ten years ago, the lake was drained and Nova Scotia geologist Don Osbourne made a study of the crater and determined a few facts.

Most importantly he noted the elliptical shape of the crater was quite rare and was clear evidence of the meteor's low angle of impact. He also found several smaller craters in the area. These are most likely fragments of the meteor that were projected away and out of the crater at impact.

I'm afraid I couldn't find any ghost stories attached to this crater so I must categorize this location in the realm of the weird, rather than the occult. Still, it is wicked cool to think that a meteor that freaking large struck Nova Scotia so very long ago.

Does anyone remember in *Armageddon*, when that group of oil-well drillers flew into outer space to fight a hit-and-run asteroid? I mean, where in the heck was Bruce Willis when we needed him most?

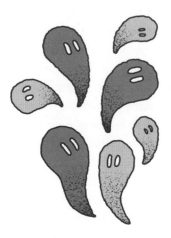

13: The Ghosts of Haliburton House
44.988796°N 64.14166°W

THE HALIBURTON HOUSE, BUILT IN 1835, would be a lovely place to visit even if the ghost of its former owner, Judge Thomas Chandler Haliburton, did not haunt the building.

Thomas Haliburton was well known back in the mid-1800s. He had built himself a reputation as a successful businessman, an honest judge, and a popular writer of fiction including the serial adventures of his beloved Sam Slick character.

In 1816 he married Louisa Neville and from 1826 to 1829 he served as the representative of Annapolis Royal in the Nova Scotia House of Assembly.

Oddly enough, when he finally decided to retire in 1856, he moved to England and served as a British Member of Parliament. He kept on writing—which is usually what we old writers can be counted on doing—and he was awarded an honorary degree from Oxford University for his efforts in literature. He passed away on August 27, 1865, at his home known as Gordon House and was buried in the Isleworth Churchyard.

So why then, does the ghost of Thomas Haliburton still continue to haunt his home, Haliburton House, here in Windsor, Nova Scotia?

The Piper of Piper's Pond

Mind you, this isn't the only ghost that is reputed to haunt the area surrounding Haliburton House.

I have already told the story that ghost-story tellers most often like to relate, concerning a young piper's heartbreaking demise, in my first Nova Scotia ghost-story collection, *Haunted Harbours: Ghost Stories From Old Nova Scotia,* but let me run through it quickly for you now.

It seems that a young Highland piper by the name of Jamie Donaldson made a pact with a young unmarried girl whom he was courting.

"Meet me by the pond," he told her. "And the two of us can run off together and be married. I have had enough of living a lonely soldier's life."

And Donnalee Jenkins, which was the young girl's name, agreed to Jamie's proposition.

Sadly, though, young Jamie was delayed by a vigilant sergeant. By the time that Jamie made it out to the pond Donnalee had lost heart. She had assumed that he was jilting her and she walked into the water of the pond until it covered her head and she did not re-emerge.

When Jamie finally arrived he could see her dead body floating out there in the heart of the pond. He marched around the pond, playing a lament or a pibroch upon his bagpipes. After marching six times around the pond he walked on into the water to join his one true love in whatever realm lay waiting beyond the here and now.

The storytellers love to tell how if you go out by the pond on a moonlit night and walk about it for six times, or seven times, or even thirteen times, depending on whatever mathematics that storyteller is relying upon, the ghost of young Jamie will rise up out of the water and play you a last long lament.

Thomas Haliburton never wrote down the story, although Nova Scotia's most noted folklorist, Helen Creighton, collected it and people still tell it over at Haliburton House, especially close to Halloween.

Only I did not want to tell you about that story but; rather, I wanted to talk to you about the ghost of Thomas Halliburton himself. Apparently, there is a secret panel in the wall of the main reception hall that the ghost often uses to make surreptitious entrances. However, on certain nights his ghost has been seen pushing his big smiling Joker-like face right through the wallpaper of the main reception hall.

Maybe he's just being a really good host?

SECTION 3
Northern Shore
& Cape Breton

14: The Drummer Boy of Ghost Lake
45°37'09.0"N 61°36'10.9"W

APPROXIMATELY ONE MILE NORTHEAST FROM the little village of Monastery, bordered by the paved stretch of Highway 104 and the winding Sunrise Trail, is a small body of water that according to historians was once known as Tracadie Lake. These days, the lake is more commonly known as Jacksons Lake, however some of the older local storytellers and fishermen still refer to that small body of water as Ghost Lake.

In 1758 the British forces at Fort Louisbourg planned to attack Fort Beauséjour, located very close to the border of Nova Scotia and New Brunswick. Since ships were not plentiful enough to carry all of the troops, some were carried to the Canso Strait and then left to march on foot. These troops were to keep the English ships in sight at all times while making their way towards Fort Beauséjour.

Once across the Strait they marched onward and they soon came to Tracadie Lake, overlooking St. George's Bay. Here they set up camp to train for the possibility of battle. The army is a little bit like school that way. You are always getting ready for some big test. During the day the troops practiced in their bright red uniforms and at night their drums and music added an eerie atmosphere to the previously tranquil area.

The local Indigenous peoples were quite fearful of their presence and were calling upon the great spirit of Glooscap when the British forces departed. However, even long after the British had left the region the Mi'kmaq could still hear the pounding of a drum beating in the distance. Elders swore it was the evil spirits of the British enemy coming to haunt them. Some even believed the drumming sounds were caused by the spirit of a soldier killed in the battle at Fort Beauséjour returning to the site where they had spent their last peaceful night among the living.

Since then, no matter what maps may reveal, the lake has been known as "Ghost Lake" to locals and storytellers and those folks who have lived long enough to remember the old stories will tell you this one, of the drummer boy of Ghost Lake.

Under the Ghost Moon

Ghost Lake was an awfully hard old place to live next to. There were hordes of black flies that would drink your veins dry and squadrons of deerfly that would chew the meat from off of your bones.

There was a young British drummer boy named Brandon who served there with the local British contingent. Drumming was a job usually given to young boys in the army to keep them out of trouble long enough for them to grow old enough to know better, only Brandon was impatient, as young boys often are. He rushed the beat of his drum and suppertime never came soon enough. Things just couldn't happen fast enough to please that boy.

He wanted to be a better drummer and he wanted to be a sergeant and he wanted to be rich and he wanted all of the cake and all of the potatoes and he didn't want to have to wait for anything at all.

One night he crept out under the late-August light of the ghost moon to practice his drumming where he would not disturb anybody's sleep and, because he was young and impatient and just a little bit foolish, he swore that he would give anything just so long as he never had to wait for anything again.

Well sir, that big old ghost moon was listening to the boy's complaining and that moon whispered a question to the blowing north wind who whispered it back again to the old man who lives beneath the North Mountain who hollered the question out loud just for the fun of it down his cold mountain well and when that question had gone down that well far enough, the Devil himself came up and gave a listen.

"Hey boy," the Devil said to Brandon. "That is some awfully fine drum banging, even if you are rushing the beat sometimes."

"What do you know about drumming?" Brandon rudely asked. "You probably wouldn't know what a stick was for if it fell off of a tree and hit you on the head."

Now, I don't know if that drummer boy was just that stupid that he did not recognize the Devil his own self when he met him right in the middle of a good old-fashioned story, or if he was just being rude for the sheer sake of working on his rudeness, but the Devil didn't like it one little bit. The Devil snapped his fingers and two long golden drumsticks grew out of his hands. Then he grinned and a full-sized set of drums set up right in front of him.

"Just watch this," the Devil said.

And that old Devil started laying it down and picking it up, starting out with a basic single-stroke roll, nodding his head in time and then picking up speed. He started alternating that single stroke with a triple-stroke bounce roll and right on into a fast-paced buzz roll—and I know that all of these drumming terms probably mean next to nothing to most of you folks, so let's just say that old Devil was drumming the heck out of those drums.

"How's that for drumming, Sonny Jim?" the Devil asked Brandon.

"That's not bad for a beginner," the drummer boy replied. "But let me take a crack at those skins."

The drummer boy already had a pair of drumsticks in his hands because he never left home without his drumsticks and he started in on that Devil's drum rolling out a fast paradiddle and a buzz roll that sounded like a woodpecker with a bad case of the hiccups. Then he started gaining speed and power. First he drummed out thunder and then he drummed out lightning. He drummed out a hard rain on a corrugated tin roof. He drummed out gunpowder and earthquakes and avalanches rolling downhill. He drummed out the heartbeat of a young girl who has just met her one true love. He drummed out a hanged man's last walk and the walk of a farmer coming home from the field and finally he wound it all up by drumming out a soldier coming home from the war.

"That's exactly what I am going to do some day," the drummer boy told that old Devil. "I am going to go on home from this war business and my momma is going to bake me a butter cake and serve it up with a tall cool glass of milk."

"That's what you think," said the Devil. "You aren't going anywhere but right where you are."

The Devil waved his hands in a funny kind of way and those drumsticks grew down into tree roots that wrapped right around the drummer boy's legs and he stood there stuck and feeling more than just a little bit stupid at ever trying to play games with the Devil.

At least that is how I heard the story told—and what they say is that you can still hear the sound of that drummer boy drumming along the shores of Ghost Lake—and I don't care what they call that lake nowadays, that drummer boy is out there still.

Why don't you take a visit there some night and have a listen?

15: The Lonely Ghosts Of Broughton
46°4′52.38″N 59°57′48.69″W

YOU WOULD NOT KNOW IT to look at it, but the little once-upon-a-town of Broughton—situated between the towns of Mira Gut and Birch Grove, just about twelve miles east of the community of Sydney, Cape Breton—was once considered a booming little industrial town that was far ahead of its time.

Broughton was one of the very first planned towns in Canada. A map will show you how the streets and avenues of the little town were neatly laid out in carefully organized rectangles, stretching out on both sides of what was supposed to become the region's largest coal mine.

An undeveloped coal deposit in the Loon Lake area caught the attention of a British mining engineer by the name of Thomas Lancaster along with a British coal mine owner by the name of Colonel Horace Mayhew, and his oldest son, Horace Dixon Mayhew Jr., who worked together to found the rather loftily titled Cape Breton Coal, Iron and Railway Company in the year 1905.

"We'll make ourselves a bleeding fortune," Colonel Mayhew said.

"Are you sure about that, Dad?" Mayhew Jr. asked.

"Certainly he's sure," Thomas Lancaster replied. "How can we lose?"

The two men hired an architect by the name of William Harris to design and built a town that they believed would eventually hold over ten thousand citizens. The two partners raised approximately $12 million (about $50 million today) from a half a dozen gullible British speculators. Unfortunately, the bulk of the initial investment was spent on laying out the network of streets, and construction of homes for the townsfolk, as well as several overly ostentatious public buildings.

Yes sir and ma'am, Mayhew and Lancaster were aiming to impress the hordes of people they believed would move into the town of Broughton. They even built a huge luxury hotel which they called The Broughton Arms and which was known to be the most luxurious hotel east of Montreal.

Believe it or not, the Broughton Arms was one of *two* hotels Mayhew and Lancaster had built for the use of visitors who, it would turn out, never arrived.

You see, Mayhew and Lancaster were forced to make use of that revolving door just one year later in 1906. Unfortunately they had built the streets and built the houses and built the collier facilities and then they went bankrupt before they could get the trains running to Broughton to bring the citizens to the town and to eventually deliver the coal that these citizens would eventually unearth to the marketplace. Basically, Broughton was a town that was built before people were ready to move in.

Mayhew Jr. took the whole situation rather hard. He just couldn't bear the shame of the bankruptcy and he shot himself with his own hunting rifle.

Colonel Mayhew and Thomas Lancaster fled back to England, shrouded in sorrow as well as a cloud of scandalous embarrassment. Mayhew landed on his feet though, going back into the coal business with his remaining sons.

It wasn't until the onset of the First World War, in the year 1914, when the little Nova Scotia town of Broughton received a much-needed shot in the arm. Nearly 1,200 soldiers of the 185th Cape Breton Highlanders set up a training camp and headquarters in Broughton, using the uninhabited houses as barracks.

Unfortunately, the Broughton Arms burned right to the ground on April 1916, during a rather boisterous weekend-long celebration.

By the end of the war the town was nearly deserted. As of 2001 there were only twenty-four citizens still living in Broughton and right now the town looks as if the Highlanders had actually fought the Kaiser's troops right there in its empty streets. The buildings are in ruins and the paved roads have long given way to gravel and the forest has run rampant through what is left of the town.

Still, the old people who know things that folks don't often care to talk about will tell you that you ought to stay out of the ghost town of Broughton after nightfall. Shapes are still seen moving through the ruins. Some believe that the remorseful ghost of Horace Dixon Mayhew Jr. haunts the little town that could have been.

Besides Mayhew Jr., back in 2017 a group of local paranormal investigators known as Haunts From The Cape spent an evening there and picked up a strange and eerie voice on an electronic listening device known as an "echo box." It is believed to be the ghost of one of the soldiers of the 185th Cape Breton Highlanders.

"Who's there?" the investigator called out. "Did you live here? Were you a resident of the town?"

"No," the voice came through the echo box. "I was a soldier."

Why don't you go and listen for yourself—but again, this is *not* a trip for a casual hiker. Make certain you bring along a compass or a GPS to ensure that you don't get lost. Some bug spray would be a good plan as well.

16: The Ghost Train of Barrachois

46°8′29.56″N 60°26′1.43″W

THE FIRST TIME I READ about the Barrachois ghost train, I just had to look deeper into it. I grew up in a railroad town. If I wanted to buy groceries, I had to cross the railroad tracks. If I wanted to go to school, I had to cross the railroad tracks. The tracks actually cut our little town into two separate pieces and there wasn't a single day of my early life when I did not have to stand and wait while a train crossed in front of me.

Mind you, I still grin every time I see a freight train rolling by—but a ghost train, now that's something else entirely. The sheer novelty captured my undivided attention. There are dozens of ghost ships in Nova Scotia, and hundreds of ghost houses—but how often do you run into an honest-to-*chugga-chugga-choo-choo* ghost train?

So let me tell you about the Barrachois ghost train.

The people who lived on a certain hill outside of Barrachois, Cape Breton, used to talk about a long black passenger train that rolled past the gate of a certain farmhouse without making a sound. It never stopped. It just rolled straight on past that farmhouse gate. All anyone could see was gouts of smoke arising from the belly of the train, spewing into the cold December air.

"It looked like a big black shadow of a gigantic worm crawling across the sky," one man swore.

The train wasn't scheduled to pass there. It never left the Sydney station. It was more along the lines of a dream of a train— except this train wasn't only seen by a single dozing farmer. Rather, this ghost train was seen by dozens of people. It became a bit of an event around the settlement. People gathered outside of the farm, watching as that long black train rolled past the farm gate without making the slightest sound.

That was the weird part of the situation. Like I said, I grew up with trains in my life and let me tell you that they are anything but silent. Trains make an awful lot of noise. I am talking maximum-decibel nuclear kettledrum thunder.

Only this particular train did not make a sound as it rolled on past the farm gate, every evening precisely at seven o'clock.

"You could set your watch by it," one witness said. "I'm pretty sure a few of us actually did."

The only person who didn't bother to come out and look at the ghost train was the farmer Bertram Littlefield, who hadn't been outside to watch since the railroad started running by his farm.

"I don't care if it's a ghost train, a mule train, or a whole-bag-full-of-gravy train," Bertram Littlefield said. "It makes too much darned noise. It frightens my horses and it addles the eggs and it frets the milk cow dry as sunburned bone."

"Don't you want to see it?" one of his neighbours asked him.

"No, I do not want to see it," Bertram Littlefield replied. "I've got too much work to do. I'm a farmer, remember? You used to be a farmer too."

"I'm still a farmer," the neighbour said. "I just like to watch the ghost train go by, is all."

The ghost train itself was totally black, but the windows were clearly lit. There is some argument about whether or not any passengers could be seen through the windows. Some say that the train appeared to be absolutely empty of life, while others swear that there were faces at each of the windows, staring blindly out into the night.

Whether empty or full of life, the train maintained its seven o'clock vigil for a solid month, all December long, and let me tell you this: the snow fell heavy that year and it was early in coming and long in staying on.

"The old woman was plucking her snow geese all winter long that year," one old farmer noted. "There was nothing out there but cool and white, just as far as the eye could see."

"I blame it on that darned ghost train," the old farmer's son said. "That train brings the winter snow nearly every year."

"It's only been the one year," the old farmer replied. "There isn't any kind of every about it. No, sir. The way I see things, it's the other way around. The train doesn't bring the snow. It's the snow that brings the train."

Now, whether the train brought the snow or the snow brought the train, death walked the railroad tracks that month, for on the last day of December Bertram Colton was attempting to cross the railroad tracks when his left boot stuck fast in the deep snow. It was early in the morning and there was no one else about when a steam locomotive pushing a great big old-fashioned snow plow came roaring down the track and it struck old Bertram as dead as last week's catch of mackerel, while he was still struggling to free himself.

Now some folks said that the train was moving too fast, but as any old-time railroader can tell you, a good head of proper speed is necessary if you want to build enough momentum to clear the tracks of a heavy winter snowfall, which is why you ought to always look carefully in both directions before attempting to cross a set of railroad tracks.

In any case, whether that train was moving too fast or old Bertram was moving too darn slowly, the local folk all agreed on what they saw. That very same night the locals all gathered around the farmhouse and waited for the long dark train to roll on by. It might have been habit. It might have been instinct. Perhaps in some sort of indefinite fashion they were simply paying homage to their fallen friend.

Whatever the reason, the entire settlement gathered out there that evening, standing around that stretch of railroad track, and as soon as the clock hit seven that long black train came rolling down out of the distance and pulled to a halt outside of Bertram's farm gate, making a hissing sound like a startled rattlesnake.

Disbelief washed over the entire crowd of spectators. The ghost train had never stopped there before. In fact, it had never stopped anywhere before now.

Some folks were scared and wanted to run and hide.

Some folks were curious and wanted to stay and watch, but no matter what they actually wanted to do the whole crowd agreed that none of them could move a single step. It was as if their feet were stuck fast in the snow.

And then the train whistle roared so loudly that distant booming harbour foghorns blushed in abject shame at their own lack of volume.

"Get back," someone shouted. "There is no telling what's going to happen next."

The farmhouse front door opened slowly with a long aching hinge creak.

And there was old Bertram.

"I thought that he was dead," somebody said.

"He ought to be dead," somebody else said. "Seeing as we buried him in the dirt, just this morning."

"It must be his ghost," the first somebody replied.

The ghost of Bertram walked right on out to the long black train, turning only once to tip his fine Sunday derby at the crowd, just as if he was strolling on his way to church. Then old ghost-Bertram stepped up onto the boarding ladder of the thirteenth passenger car. The door of the passenger car swung open and a porter who looked to be made completely out of shadow and smoke tipped his hat as Bertram walked inside.

The ghost train was never seen again, but some nights you can still hear the sound of its lonely call whistling, echoing over the woods and the fields of Barrachois.

17: The Golden Arm

46.2499° N, 60.2900° W

BRAS D'OR LAKE ISN'T ACTUALLY a lake at all.
Technically, it is an inland sea composed of a mixture of
salt and fresh water and connected to the Atlantic Ocean
through natural channels: the Great Bras d'Or Channel north of
Boularderie Island and the Little Bras d'Or Channel to south—
which both connect the northeastern arm of the lake to the
Cabot Strait—as well as the man-made Strait of Canso and the St.
Peters Canal. "Bras d'Or" means "golden arm," a reference to the
way summer sunlight gleams on the water. The Mi'kmaq refer to
the area as *Pitu'pok*, which is roughly translated as "long salt water."

The area is home to an awful lot of ghost stories including
an old legend of the ghost of a lonely Mi'kmaw man who can
sometimes be seen paddling his canoe out there in the open water
in the late hours, just before dusk. Some folks tell you that he
has lost someone near and dear to his heart and he is doomed

to forever search, while other folks will tell you the man is lost himself. Still other folks will tell you of a great Spanish sailing ship that can sometimes be seen sailing in from the sea, hunting for buried treasure.

It is beautiful area to visit and the surrounding region was declared a UNESCO Biosphere Reserve back in the year 2011. There are plenty places to stay, but if you are looking for somewhere to camp then I'd recommend the Arm of Gold Campground.

I spent a weekend a mile or two away from the campground at a friend's cottage one summer, several years ago, and I asked my friend just why the lake was called "the golden arm" and this is the story he told me.

The Golden Arm

There are stories that are told all across the world, in a whole lot of different ways, and this is one of them. This is the story of Marcel's golden arm.

Many years ago, in the Bras d'Or region of Nova Scotia, there lived a farmer by the name of Marcel Tooker, who didn't have much luck to his name. He eked out a living growing bitter turnips and ghost-white parsnips. He didn't like to eat that stuff, you understand. Parsnips and turnips were all Marcel could grow. He made do with what he had. Still, it irked him whenever he'd see his neighbour, Old Man Howley.

If you asked Marcel why he hated Old Man Howley he'd just grunt and say, "I don't know." The truth was Marcel was jealous of Old Man Howley's wealth. It wasn't as if Old Man Howley bragged all that much. In fact, he didn't talk to Marcel at all. The honest-to-wishing-bone truth of it was that Old Man Howley wouldn't bother saying, "it sure is raining" even if the sky was bucketing down on the both of them. I guess more than anything Marcel was frog-green envious over Old Man Howley's golden arm.

Some folks said Old Man Howley was a soldier who'd saved the life of a king in a battle and lost his arm in a cannon blast. The king was so grateful to Old Man Howley he gave him that golden arm in place of a medal.

Other folks say Old Man Howley made a deal with the Devil for that gold. They said come Judgment Day the Devil would cast Old Man Howley down into the flames of Perdition itself. Some folks swore Old Man Howley was so darned cheap he preferred to wear his gold on his arm instead of paying a bank to hold it for him. Some folks say a lot of things but Marcel hated Old Man Howley more than any man on the planet had the right to go hating on any other man you care to mention.

He just didn't like him, is all.

So one night, Marcel Tooker crept out of his tumbledown old shack and skittered across his parsnip and turnip field. He lifted a leg over the zigzag of Old Man Howley's split-rail fence and slunk across his neighbour's yard, right on up to the back door.

A little voice deep down inside of Marcel's better sense whispered that he ought not to do this thing he was thinking on doing, but he went and did it anyway. He pried that door open with a piece of cold iron and tiptoed inside.

He had a big bull's-eye lantern with him, the kind used by hunters and treasure seekers.

Marcel Tooker walked up to Old Man Howley's bedside. He stared at Old Man Howley sleeping there in his big old brass bed. The old man had one bad eye and a little trickle of snore-spit snail-crawing out of the corner of his mouth and he was snoring softly, kind of like the sound that a big old luna moth might make while it was sawing up moonbeams to build itself a house with.

Marcel didn't care a lick about Old Man Howley's bad eye or snoring problem. He was too busy staring at that big old golden arm. It was huge this close up and probably worth about a billion or two dollars and Marcel got to thinking about what he could do with all that gold.

Marcel was so busy thinking about spending the gold he didn't notice Old Man Howley wake on up and try to strangle the life out of him. Then Marcel reached back behind himself and grabbed up a kindling hatchet from the bedroom fireplace and swung it down right smack onto Old Man Howley's head.

It felt like Marcel had split a big old coconut. Old Man Howley's eyes opened wide and closed shut and he sank into the pillow, his face settling into a pig-eating-corn kind of a smile, like he knew some sort of a secret joke that he was taking down into the deep dark swallow of death.

Old Man Howley was as dead as the dirt of an unmarked grave. Marcel didn't take much notice on account of the way he kept staring at that big golden arm. He could see that arm wasn't anything Old Man Howley wore. That gold arm grew right out of Old Man Howley's shoulder bone. Marcel could even see the way that the gold had worked its way in and around Old Man Howley's neck bones.

Marcel couldn't help himself.

He just had to touch it.

He reached down and touched that golden arm and the gold oozed on up over Marcel's fingertips and crawled up Marcel's right arm. It felt a little bit like Marcel was watching a great big old golden snake slowly gulping down a long pink five-fingered tree frog.

Faster than you can say "swallow," that golden arm had crawled on up Marcel's very own arm and for the very first time in his life he knew just how hard and heavy a thing it could be, to have to wear a great big old golden arm for the rest of his days.

And that whole time Old Man Howley lay there on his bed, dead and smiling.

Marcel turned and kicked open the bedroom door that had swung back shut. He ran down Old Man Howley's back hallway and past the kitchen where Old Man Howley's servant was coming out of, waving a meat cleaver and yelling out like all of the angels of the last day where climbing out of the kitchen oven.

Only Marcel didn't pay that servant any heed at all. He kicked down the front door with one scared boot and kept on running, clearing the split-rail fence at a single bound that would've qualified him for a solid gold medal in the Olympics track and field competition.

He ran out into the woods, looking back over his shoulder on account of he was afraid that somebody might be following him—like maybe the ghost of Old Man Howley—which was why he ran face-first into the biggest swamp oak in the whole entire Bras d'Or woods.

Well sir, when Marcel hit that big old swamp oak his brand-new golden arm swung up and caught him right on the flat of his forehead and knocked him out colder than a fresh-frozen mackerel. He hit that swamp oak so hard the leaves fell off its branches, covering Marcel's knocked-out body like a crackly golden bed quilt. Marcel lay under those freshly fallen leaves, snoring softly, a few leaves that had fallen over the lips of his mouth, shivering like they were scared of whatever was coming next.

The big golden moon looked down and just watched while everything slowly unfolded.

That was when the first call came—a big howl of a voice, haunting out over the evening breeze, coming in soft and low and booming and hollow like somebody yodelling into the belly of an empty rain barrel.

"I want my gooooooolden arm!" the ghost of Old Man Howley howled out.

Marcel opened up his eyes, like a pair of rudely snapped window blinds. He felt the dirt bugs crawling all over him and he felt the night breeze rattling over those freshly fallen oak leaves and he felt that big old heavy golden arm laying crossed over on top of his chest with enough weight to crush his lungs to stillness. Marcel skootched himself into the fallen leaves and tried to sort of seal flipper up a bit of dirt with his one good hand to hopefully try to hide himself under.

And that was when that second call rang out.

"I want my GOOOOOOOOLDEN ARM!!" the ghost of Old Man Howley howled.

Thunder boomed from a long away, like a storm coming

on, only Marcel wasn't certain that it wasn't the sound of his
stampeding heart. He skootched down even further, hiding himself
in the dirt and whispering about as much of the Lord's Prayer
as he could remember, only the words stuck to his lips as if he
couldn't manage to spit them out.

And that was when the third call rang out.

"I WANT MY GOOOOOOOOOOOOOOOOOLLLLLDEN
ARM!!!" the ghost of Old Man Howley thundered.

And that was when Marcel sat up.

"Well, take it!" he shouted.

Nobody knows just what happened to Marcel that night.

The townsfolk found Marcel's body lying there in the Bras
d'Or woods, half-chewed by a weasel, a few raccoons, and a bear
with a toothache. They wondered to themselves what brought
this poor man to such a bitter end. They wondered why he'd tried
to bury himself beneath the roots of this big old swamp oak. But
mostly, they wondered what the flapjacks had happened to Marcel
Tooker's missing right arm.

Now that is just how my friend told the story to me, and to
this day the folks who still remember will tell you there are certain
nights you ought to stay out of the woods out beyond Marcel
Tooker's little shack; and if you push them to it they'll tell you that
come every autumn the leaves of the swamp oak are as bright and
gold-coloured as a golden arm.

18: A Miracle At Tim Hortons

46°15'2.99"N 60°17'19.86"W

NOW I DO NOT KNOW about you folks, but speaking for me, my most significant miracle that I have ever experienced at a Tim Hortons shop was pretty nearly any time that I managed to win myself a free Tim Hortons donut, thanks to the heavenly blessed Roll Up The Rim contest. The muffins are nice as well, but there is something that is truly wonderful about the taste of a Tim Hortons maple dip donut—especially when it is free.

I know that a free SUV would have been a whole lot better, economically speaking—but hey, who am I to argue with a free maple dip donut?

Still, any sort of a discussion about weird and eerie events in Nova Scotia would not be complete without a mention of the unexpected appearance of the Savior Jesus Christ at a Little Bras d'Or Tim Hortons.

Located just off of Highway 5, perfect for drive-by coffee runs, the Little Bras d'Or Tim Hortons was apparently the scene of a heavenly visitation from the Lord. It was September 1998, and a couple driving down the highway noticed that the sky was illuminated with sunbeams that looked almost heavenly.

"It looked like one of those pictures you see in a big old-fashioned Bible. You know, with the beams of light cascading down like Klingon-killing phaser beams," the husband said. "I just had one of those weird kind of feelings that I just had to stop and have a better look. I hit the brakes and stopped right in the middle of the highway. If there had been a big old truck coming up right behind us I guess that I would have been shopping for either a brand new car or a brand new double-sized coffin come Monday, but I guess that we were just lucky, or else somebody was watching out for us overhead."

"The light beams were focusing right down onto the bricks between two of the big panes of window glass," the wife added. "It almost looked as if the good Lord Jesus Christ his-own-self was looking at us right out from the bricks of the Tim Hortons wall."

"It was just like watching Captain Kirk beam down from the USS *Enterprise*," the husband said.

"Oh you just think that everything that happens has something to do with *Star Trek*," the wife said. "You know that life doesn't work that way, don't you?"

"Well, explain this," the husband said, flipping his old flip-top cellphone out and calling up his brother to tell him about what he had just seen.

Pretty soon the word had got around, which doesn't really take all that much effort in a town with a population of 135. Basically, what happened is somebody told two friends and then those two told two friends who also two friends and faster than you can say "Faberge," the word had really got around.

People started showing up by the carload, and then dozens of cars began to show up. The parking lot for the world-famous fast-food restaurant, A&K Lick-A-Chick (386 Park Road), proved to be an ideal viewing spot, although there were also crowds of the curious clustered about the suddenly sanctified Tim Hortons.

"It is just amazing and it actually gave me goosebumps," said nearby Groves Point resident Margie Keeping. "The image was a little blurry but up close when you move a little bit back you can see the Lord."

The word continued to spread across Nova Scotia like a summer wildfire and pretty soon the parking lots and side of the road were crammed solid with cars. Cashiers at both the A&K Lick-A-Chick as well as the Tim Hortons said that it was pretty good for business.

"People just smelled the chicken while they were standing out there and looking," said one Lick-A-Chick employee. "They just couldn't help themselves. They came on in and ordered some good fried chicken."

Lori Steele of nearby Glace Bay had heard the rumour from a friend while she was out shopping and drove to Little Bras d'Or immediately, just to see what the fuss was all about. When she got there she could not believe her eyes.

"I just can't believe it," Lori Steele said. "It is the face of Christ—his hair, his beard, and his robe—it's all there."

As the crowds began to thicken, onlookers continued to show up. This time they brought along lawn chairs and coolers and the whole area began to look a little less like a public thoroughfare and a little bit more like a walk-in rock festival. People grew careless and bold as a multitude of curious spectators began to pull up into convenient driveways, even parking their cars upon people's front lawns.

Meanwhile the word of the miraculous Roll Up The Rim miracle had begun to spread nationwide as the radio, television, and internet got into the action.

Worried about the tumultuous crowds growing even larger and more uncontrollable, the owner of the coffee shop, as well as the authorities, decided upon a simple measure. A stepladder and a brand-new light bulb to replace the one that had initially burned out was all that it took to exorcise the image of the Lord Jesus Christ.

Now, I should tell you that the Tim Hortons currently in that location is *not* the very same Tim Hortons where the caffeinated miracle occurred; that holy Tim Hortons was torn down in the summer of 2016. The owners say it was nothing more than a simple update and a much-needed renovation; however, some of the local folk feel differently.

In a CBC report, long-time Little Bras d'Or resident Kim Whitby wondered what had happened to the blessed bricks upon which the Lord had apparently shown himself: "Whether or not the Jesus bricks are here or gone or if they were taken out individually and kept to the side, I just don't know," she said.

When the reporter asked about the whereabouts of the so-called "Jesus bricks" at the mobile Tim Hortons that was filling in until the new facility was open for business, all that they could tell her was, "God only knows."

I expect He does.

19: The Critter of Cranberry Lake
46°14′24″N, 60°16′27″W

THIS PARTICULAR WEIRD LOCATION TOOK me a little while to track down. It seems that there are at least forty Cranberry Lakes of all shapes and sizes here in Nova Scotia, not to mention a few cranberry bogs. Still, this one specific Cranberry Lake that I am referring to is a long skinny dangle of water, running about a mile long. This Cranberry Lake is located just a few kilometres northwest of Sydney, and is the home to Cape Breton's very own lake lizard.

Nobody really has given this particular critter a name. We Maritimers leave it to those western folk to be throwing around multi-syllabic names such as Ogopogo, Manipogo, Igopogo, Memphremagog and not to mention Kempenfelt Kelly. No sir, the folks in Cape Breton just referred to the Cranberry Lake Critter as "that big, funny-smelling fishy thing down there in the water."

It took some looking around to hunt up a story attached to this lake monster. Helen Creighton mentioned it in passing in her famous *Bluenose Ghosts* (Nimbus Publishing, 1957) and Andrew Hebda, zoology curator for the Nova Scotia Museum, mentions it in his publication *The Serpent Chronologies* (NSM, 2015)—however, the story itself has remained nearly as elusive as the lake monster itself.

So let me tell it the way that I heard it told.

Back in 1927, Alan Macabee had been following the tracks of three or four wandering cows. He wasn't concerned about the possibility of losing these cows, nor was he worried any of his neighbours might try and steal those cows. This was Cape Breton, after all. Folks were more interested in helping each other, rather than helping themselves.

It was a fine evening for a stroll, and it was a good excuse to tell his wife, Jolene, who had her hands full with his one-year-old son, Alan, whom everyone called Little Al. Cape Breton or not, Alan Macabee enjoyed a little peace and quiet whenever he could find the time and opportunity for it.

"I'm going to go looking for those cows," Alan Macabee told his wife. "I think they might have wandered down to the Cranberry Lake for a drink of cold fresh lake water. I'd better round them up before they founder. I'll be sure to be back before the dark falls."

"Sure," his wife wryly replied. "And you'd best be sure to see you don't wander down to Henry's Pub for a drink of cold never-you-mind, or you'll sleep in the woodshed."

Alan Macabee dutifully nodded and carefully closed the door behind himself before walking out towards Cranberry Lake.

"Sure, and a long cold drink is what them cows would be looking for," he told himself. "I'll find all four of them standing knee-deep in the water and dewclaw-deep in mud, nibbling on lake weeds and enjoying the cool night breeze."

Sure enough, that was where they were, knee-deep in the water, only they weren't mooing contentedly. Now, some of you city folk most likely figure that mooing is all the noise a cow can make, but cows make an awful lot of different sort of noises. They'll snort when they're short-tempered and if they're hungry they'll moo loudly and when they're feeling happy and satisfied they'll low contentedly, which is actually kind of deeper-sounding than your average run-of-the-mill moo.

And when one of the herd has been taken by a bear or a pack of coyotes, those cows will breathe deep from the bottom of their belly and they will bellow just as a loud as a roll of summer thunder—and that was what those cattle were doing when Alan Macabee came walking upon them.

He didn't walk for long, mind you. As soon as Alan heard them bellowing he kicked his old work boots into a run and got to the lakeshore just as the monster rose up out of the deep. Alan had never seen anything like this before in his whole entire lifetime. He stopped short, with one boot half kicked off and the other slowly sinking into the mud of the shoreline.

The critter came roaring up out of the depths of Cranberry Lake. It had a long, bluish-green serpentine body with a head about the size of a steam shovel bucket all feathered with a tangle of gigantic catfish-like whiskers. The beast's eyes were about as red as a bunch of mid-September cranberries.

In as quick a time as it took to read that last sentence the Cranberry Lake Critter opened its mouth as wide as if its jaws were double-jointed and bit down into the haunches of the cow that had ventured out deepest into the lake. The Critter leaned its long neck backwards like a fisherman trying to pull a monster pike up out of the water, before vanishing back into the depths of Cranberry Lake—cow and all.

"Come on, cows," Alan said, wading out into the water, all the while looking over his shoulder nervously just in case that big old monster came roaring back up out of the water for a second helping. Alan had the feeling that somebody had sneaked up and painted a great big old FREE TWO-LEGGED DESSERT sign on the back of his shirt and he wasn't exactly sure if that beast could read or not. Alan got the cows back to the pasture and then ran home and told his wife what he had seen down by the lake.

"I hope that woodshed is comfortable," Henrietta said.

"Because you're sleeping in it tonight, for the next three nights running—and if you ever come home again with a story like that on your ale-stained lips then you might want to seriously consider building onto that woodshed."

Alan Macabee spent the rest of his life telling his lake monster story to nearly everyone who would listen to him long enough to laugh out loud.

It wasn't until his son, Little Al, had grown into a fully grown farmer that folks would come to believe it as truth.

That's right.

Two dozen years later, Little Al Macabee had just driven his brand new 1957 Chevy pickup truck down to the lake shore to do a little beach fishing when the Critter of Cranberry Lake decided to put in a surprise appearance.

"He came up out of the water like a missile, shot from out of a submarine," Little Al said. "Just the way my Dad had told me."

The Critter came and went without even so much as a growl or even a lowing. He probably was a little disappointed that there hadn't been any cows around.

Cows or not, folks took Little Al's sighting a little more seriously than they had taken his father's. A group of local hunters made their way down to Cranberry Lake, with shotguns and hunting rifles and even a few old-fashioned whaling harpoons; planning to go all Ahab on that poor old cow-eating Critter.

As far as I know that Cranberry Lake Critter was never seen again. It might be that all of those shotguns and harpoons scared it off. Either that, or Henry's Pub has one heck of a stuffed-head trophy hanging over the bar right now.

20: The Phantom Ship of Northumberland Strait

Located anywhere in the coastal waters between Amherst and Baddeck, so set your GPS detector on maximum-wide!

I'VE READ A LOT OF stories about a lot of phantom ships—but as far as I can tell there is only one ship that's been seen in such a wide range of ocean water—that is the Northumberland Strait. Which is why I'm not listing a particular GPS coordinate for these stories—because the Phantom Ship has been seen in dozens of individual locations.

According to noted folklore historian Roland H. Sherwood's paperback *The Phantom Ship of Northumberland Strait and Other Mysteries of the Sea* (Lancelot Press, 1975), the mysterious apparition has been seen "in Richibucto, Buctoche, Shediac, Baie Verte, and Tormentine in New Brunswick; in Tignish, Summerside, Charlottetown, and Murray Harbour on Prince Edward Island; and from Wallace to Pugwash to Pictou and on to Mulgrave and beyond."

Now that's an awful lot of eye witnesses eyeballing that eerie burning ghost ship from an awful lot of different perspectives. A phenomenon as widespread as the Phantom Ship is awfully hard to explain as simply "a manifestation of oceanic phosphorescence" or possibly "methane gas rising from submarine coal beds" or "the setting of the crescent moon upon the horizon" or simply "just one too many shot glass swallows of 200 proof bootleg rum."

Certain debunk-minded sea experts have even blamed it upon squid ink. I swear to Neptune that I'm telling the absolute truth. I've read that certain scientists claim the constant sightings of a glowing phantom ship are nothing more than an optical illusion caused by the squirting of squid ink. It seems that when panicked by attack, schools of squid have been known to produce an abundance of blackish-brown phosphorescent ink. They hypothesize that the combination of wind, water current, and static electricity acts upon the glowing ink to create what appears to be the illusion of a giant phantom vessel.

Whether ghost or squid-toots, the vessel has been seen by hundreds of witnesses over the years and all of them describe it as a three-masted square rigger with burning flames leaping up the masts, aflame from keel to crow.

And don't think that every one of these witnesses have remained content to sit upon the shoreline and gawk at the flaming phantom ship as it sails on past. The very first recorded sighting of the mysterious phantom ship took place in Pictou back in 1880.

Let me tell you all about it.

It seems a three-masted, 648-ton barque set sail from Pictou, headed for Britain.

The barque was spotted later that day, becalmed just beyond the easternmost end of Pictou Island. No one was worried. The wind had died, as winds often do, and there was nothing that the captain of the ship could be expected to do about the weather, save for cursing it and wishing it'd change.

Later that night, a similar-looking three-masted vessel was spotted on the outskirts of Pictou Harbour, aflame from keel to crow—which is another way of saying that the ship was on fire from its bottom-most belly (that would be the keel), up to its uppermost reaches of the crow's nest.

"It's the barque," somebody shouted. "The barque is on fire!"

Captain Alan Graham and a hastily gathered group of volunteers fired up the captain's steam tugboat and set out to rescue any survivors that might still be on-board that flaming ship, but no matter how fast they steamed towards that eerie burning ship, it seemed to slip away just a little further whenever they seemed to be closing on it.

"I'd have better luck catching a freshly greased pig with both of my hands tied in a double sheet bend behind my back," the captain said. "The closer we get the farther it slips away."

The flaming ship pulled at least three nautical miles from the pursuing steamboat before vanishing like a popped soap bubble. Feeling mystified, the captain and his crew steamed back into Pictou, not knowing what to make of the whole situation.

Their confusion deepened when they got word the next day from an incoming ship that the missing barque had been spotted sailing through the Strait of Canso, without any trace of fire damage.

Some sailors believed the Phantom Ship originally belonged to an English privateer who'd met with success raiding the Nova Scotia coastline. After razing a small settlement, the captain gave orders to his crew to fetch the prettiest girl they could find among the ruins.

The captain took that pretty girl to his cabin and tried to have his way with her. She resisted his efforts. In the struggle an oil lamp was overturned and a roaring fire broke out on-board the ship. Captain and crew were lost in the fire and the ship wound up on the bottom of the Northumberland Strait, just off the shores of Pictou Island.

Many people have spotted the ship, even in the twenty-first century. It's often sighted in the autumn months. Some claim it's only seen just before a fierce nor'easter blows on in.

This autumn why don't you try spending a night or two in one of the many bed and breakfasts or cottages that can readily be found along the Nova Scotia shoreline bordering the Northumberland Strait?

Who knows? You might even be the very next witness to lay eyes upon the Phantom Ship of the Northumberland Strait.

21: The Dagger Woods Howler
45°35′36″N 61°50′26″W

"The Hidey-Hinder, by the gates of Hades
Overcame Daddy and took the Mama and babies
The Hidey-Hinder done took 'em good
Back to its lair, deep in Dagger Woods"
−The Stanfields (2010)

B ACK IN 2004, OUR LOCAL Word on the Street festival
held a "Pitch the Publisher" session, inviting three Maritime
publishers to sit in judgement—à la Dragons Den and/or Shark
Tank—over the pitches of several dozen local writers. The
deal was that you got about three minutes to stand up and tell
those publishers just why they could not go on living without
publishing your book. I was one of those first-pitch writers and
I stood up and I made my speech as to why I thought that I was
the best person to write a collection of local Nova Scotia ghost
stories.

"That's quite a pitch," Sandra McIntyre, who was Nimbus Publishing's managing editor back then. "Are you some kind of a stand-up comedian?"

It came down to two local publishers who flipped a coin, and Nimbus won the coin toss. That is how my very first ghost story collection, *Haunted Harbours: Ghost Stories From Old Nova Scotia*, became the very first book to be published from Halifax's Word On the Street Festival's very first Pitch the Publisher session.

So, in a way, you could say that 2004 was when I first stepped into this story. I sat down at the Nova Scotia Archives and dug up twenty-one of the very spookiest stories that I could find. Just as soon as I came across a note regarding a mysterious creature prowling through the woods just in between Antigonish and the village of Heatherton, bordering along the long empty stretches of Highway 104, heading towards Cape Breton.

I knew that I had to write a story about that particular location. Unfortunately all that I had to work with back then was a brief hazy description and a few mixed details but I dug down deep and I finally come up with a story that I entitled "The Hidey-Hinder of Dagger Woods".

The book *Haunted Harbours* came out in 2007 after three or four cover changes and a half dozen title refits. Imagine my surprise in 2010 when I got a call from Jon Landry, the lead singer from Nova Scotia's best tavern band, The Stanfields.

Let me be honest with you: the very first thing I thought to myself was, "How cool is this!"

"Hey, Steve," Jon Landry told me. "I read your story of the Hidey-Hinder of Dagger Woods and I was just so inspired that I had to write a song about it. Is that all right with you?"

Well, I could have got all of fussy but I'm a storyteller and I spend my days picking bits of bone and gristle from out of the graves of a thousand different stories and stitching them together into brand new stories all of the time. So why the heck should I have been upset about him using my words as inspiration? Besides that, it was a whole different storyline and a whole different angle and aside from the name, "Hidey-Hinder," it didn't really feel a little bit like that story of mine.

Besides, I thought that it was just freaking wicked cool to have a good old-fashioned raucous and roll band like The Stanfields singing about one of my stories. I mean, how smoking cool is that? The song is track one of The Stanfields' very first full-length CD, *The Vanguard of the Young & Reckless*, which is a heck of a name for a first CD.

What I like best about The Stanfields is the way their Celtic-inspired music combines with the Tom Waits–like gearbox voice of Jon Landry. The mixture just automatically gets your toes tapping and your right hand slapping on a tavern table, and all of a sudden you start calling out for beer and maybe howling along with the music just a little bit if the bouncers don't mind…and even if they do.

The interesting thing is that Jon and I pronounce "Hidey-Hinder" differently. When I tell the story I pronounce it so that the "Hinder" part rhymes with "find her" because I am alluding to a critter who likes to sneak up behind you; while Jon Landry sings it as if the "Hinder" part of the word is actually "hinder" as in the sense that tavern bouncers often hinder an old storyteller's desire to howl along with the band. That's it, hinder, as in get in the way of something. In any case, I sure do love me a good storytelling song, and I recommend you go on out and give a listen to The Stanfields the first chance that you get.

The Story Behind the Dagger Woods Beastie

There are several different versions of the story of the creature that lurks in Dagger Woods. Old time Gaelic storytellers love to talk about the Bochdan of Dagger Woods, a devilish creature part bogeyman and part hobgoblin who loved to scare horses and waylay travellers and murder the unsuspecting. These stories started being told back in the late 1700s when the area was first being settled.

Now Bochdans came in many shapes and sizes, often hiding in deep ponds or thick woodlands, such as Dagger Woods. Apparently, the Bochdan that was reputed to live in Dagger Woods had come from the Old Country, hidden in amongst the cargo hold of a ship full of Scottish immigrants. He used to terrify people as well as their horses with his unearthly ear-piercing screams.

Eventually, that screaming got folks to forget all about calling him a Bochdan and instead they began to refer to him as the Dagger Woods Howler. However, there is another version that is often told about the being that inhabits Dagger Woods.

Legend has it that a husband killed his wife and children in a fit of rage. The weapon he used was a pearl-handled dagger. I haven't been able to find a name for this fellow as of yet. I could make up something—say Bill or George or Periwinkle—but Antigonish storytellers who know what they are talking about refer to him as the Dagger Woods Howler.

The murderer ran into the woods, maybe to hide from pursuit or maybe to hide from his own bloodstained conscience. Some folks will tell you he hanged himself out there or else cut his own throat with the same pearl-handled dagger he'd used to assassinate his wife and children. Others will tell you he's still living out there, feeding off of fear and guilt. Whether he died and came back as a spirit or lived on as some sort of animated corpse, he's said to utter horrendous and inhuman screams that seem to almost creep up on you, closer and closer, until the Howler is close enough to grab while you are standing there petrified with fear as he drags you off into the unexplored heart of Dagger Woods.

This, then, is the part of the legend the Jon Landry song leans more upon. His version of the Hidey-Hinder has a lot more to do with a man who has lost his family. I won't tell you any more about that song. You just go and listen to it, like I already told you.

As for me, I have always leaned less towards the screaming and more towards the whole sneaking-up-on-you aspect of the Hidey-Hinder. You can go and hunt up a copy of *Haunted Harbours: Ghost Stories From Old Nova Scotia* if you want to hear my first version of the story, or you might also want to hunt up a copy of my children's picture book *Maritime Monsters: A Field Guide* (Nimbus Publishing, 2009) for another version of the story.

SECTION 4
Eastern Shore

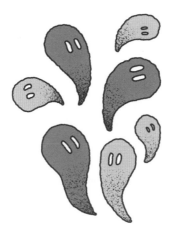

22: The Crousetown Canary

44° 14' 55" N, 64° 28' 38.9" W

THERE HAVE BEEN AN AWFUL lot of ghosts seen in the province of Nova Scotia. There have also been an awful lot of sea monsters seen in Nova Scotia. But, as far as I can manage to discover there has only been one single solitary sighting of a big old giant bird.

Let me tell you all about it.

It was a cool summer day during the month of August 2008, in the little Nova Scotia village of Crousetown, about fifteen kilometres south of the town of Bridgewater, when eighty-year-old resident Myles Rafuse was attacked by a huge unidentified black bird.

"I had quite an experience with it, I tell you," Myles Rafuse was quoted as saying. "I was going along just minding my own business, walking home from my morning church service, kicking up the dust on that old dirt road, when that bird came right at me."

Rafuse had never seen anything like it in his life before.

"I was going along and it got kind of middling warm so I took my go-to-church jacket off of my back and I carried the jacket over my arm, when all of a sudden I heard something pushing through the woods. I thought maybe it was a porcupine or a big old raccoon or even a deer, but then all of a sudden this huge black bird come straight at me on the road and made a rush at me.

"That bird was just as black as coal under the ground and he stood nearly two feet tall and just as wide and it comes at me like it thought I was something fixed for breakfast and let me tell you, mister man, that bird looked awfully mean and hungry to me. So I just kept on backing up and trying not to tangle up my feet while I was doing it and I kept on swatting at that big old bird with my jacket. I could have run faster if I had turned around, you understand, but I was afraid to turn my back on that big old black bird."

Apparently the Crousetown Canary never actually flew at all. I don't know if that bird couldn't fly or if maybe it was just too darned hot to fly that day. Either way that bird just ran straight at Myles Rafuse, running at him from the underbrush on the roadside flapping its wings partially out from its body, like somebody half opening and half closing a pair of black car doors.

"The bird made a big howling roar," Rafuse went on. "And I thought for sure it was going to get me and then it turned and veered like something had scared it and it sure wasn't me that was doing the scaring. I was too busy being scared silly to think about frightening anything off."

It might sound like an awfully silly story, but Rafuse also reported that he's taken to carrying a stout birch walking stick whenever he sets out on the long walk into town.

Myles Rafuse wasn't the only witness to report such a sighting. Seventy-three-year-old Crousetown resident Goldie Stewart told a *Chronicle Herald* reporter she'd seen the Crousetown Canary as well.

"I was out by my driveway hanging out the laundry to dry when the biggest black bird that I have ever seen swooped right down so close to me that I heard and I felt the rush of the air from its beating wings on top of my head."

Goldie Stewart had a theory as to why that big black bird attacked her like it did.

"It might have been after my long white hair to make itself a nest with," Goldie said, with a rueful chuckle. "I shooed it away and then the bird flew off over the brook and down into the woods and do you know that I haven't seen that bird back on that road since, and I sure do not want to see it ever again. It scared the living life out of me."

Goldie Stewart's hair theory might indeed be a possibility. Smaller birds will use human hair and horse hair and even cat fur, if they can find it, to build themselves a nest. Perhaps the monster bird had been thinking about building a home and settling down in the woods outside of Crousetown.

Wouldn't that have been fun?

An official of the provincial Department of Natural Resources considered several theories, that perhaps the bird might actually have been a big old raven or a cormorant flown inland or even a stooping northern goshawk.

"It sounded far too big to me to be any kind of a raven, and cormorants don't travel too far into inland forests unless they are blown off course by the wind. As for a goshawk, well that would be grey, not black," the official theorized. "Given the size of the bird and the fact that it ran at Myles Rafuse it might have been a turkey that somebody had released in the province. Turkeys have been seen in the wild once or twice in Nova Scotia and it is always possible that it got away from a nearby turkey farm. They can run pretty fast and they will even roost in trees, given the chance. Yes sir, that's the only bird I can think of that could possibly grow to that size witnesses reported it to be."

Another theory reported by several noted Canadian cryptozoologists was that the bird was a black vulture, a bird which has been occasionally spotted in Nova Scotia. Other folks believe it was a preternaturally preserved prehistoric bird such as an Archaeopteryx (extinct since the Jurassic Period) or an eastern moa (considered to be extinct since 1400 AD) or else some other long-extinct proto-bird, but I'm not so certain about that.

There haven't been any other sightings of that giant bird that some folks like to call the Crousetown Canary. I can't tell you just what it actually was, but I wonder if that cranky old bird didn't eventually wind up as the main course of some Crousetown family's Thanksgiving dinner.

Please pass the gravy, now would you?

23: The Grey Lady of Stoney Beach
44° 42′ 40.55″ N, 65° 36′ 33″ W

THERE ARE A GREAT MANY "grey ladies" who walk the shores of Nova Scotia. In fact, I could readily fill an entire book with their individual stories.

You don't believe me?

Just try some of these out for size.

How to Turn Port Into Annapolis

Back in the winter of 1604 French merchant and explorer Pierre Dugua, Sieur de Mons, and his cartographer, Samuel de Champlain, were having themselves a rough old time on the island of Saint Croix, situated between Maine and New Brunswick.

"Whose idea was it to settle on this festering cold sore of an island, anyway?" de Mons asked.

"I am pretty sure that it was your idea in the first place," Champlain replied, "and if you ask me—or even if you don't ask me, it was a really stinkpot of a bad idea. It is so cold out this morning that the codfish are growing their very own fur coats and gloves."

"Never mind the cold," de Mons said. "It is so blasted windy here on this island that my best hen laid the very same egg three times in a row this morning. I had to run out and catch the egg before it blew back in for the fourth time running."

They were both joking and trying to make the best of a bad situation, but there was nothing funny about what was going on. Since they had built their first settlement here on the barren and exposed island of St. Croix, nearly eighty of the colonists had died of scurvy and exposure to the cold.

"Do you know what I think?" Champlain asked. "I think that it is time we found a better place to live."

So the two of them and the remaining crew climbed back onto their ships and sailed until they reached the town now known as Annapolis Royal—only back then it was called Port Royal. Here, on Stoney Beach, they built a large and cozy sanctuary that they called "The Habitation."

"Habitation?" Champlain said. "What kind of a name is that?"

"I am going to call our settlement Port Royal," de Mons said. "You write it on the map—and in a few hundred years people will think that you named everything around here."

"It is good to be the mapmaker," Champlain replied. "You should have practiced your printing a little harder back in school."

They built Port Royal, starting with the stoutly fortified Habitation and growing from there. However, a decade or so later, British forces burned the fortifications down and claimed the spot for their own, keeping the name of Port Royal. The fort changed hands several times until eventually the settlement was moved a little further upstream to the site of the present-day town of Annapolis Royal.

The Annapolis Royal Grey Lady has been seen upon that stony beachfront at least a half a dozen recorded times since then.

The story goes something like this.

It seems that a certain young captain met and fell in love with a beautiful woman in a long grey dress during a sea voyage. Now, there is nothing wrong with meeting and falling in love with a beautiful any sort of a person—but the problem was that the captain was already married and had children as well and more important than either his wife or his children was his personal reputation.

The captain did not want the story of his illicit seaborne romance to be known by too many people. He felt certain that he could trust his crew to keep the secret, because they would not dare to betray their captain, not as long as they wanted to keep on working and getting paid on-board his ship.

However, once the story of his love got onto land, the captain would have very little control of what might be said about his deeds.

"Let us go for a walk in the woods," he told this beautiful young woman. "For I would like to be alone with you for a little while longer, away from the eyes of other men."

The hard-edged truth of it was that all he was telling her was that he wanted to get her to where there would be no witnesses. So the two of them walked off into the woods and when the captain returned there was no sign of the woman in the long grey dress.

The missing woman's ghost was sighted shortly after the incident occurred. Two local men first saw her. She was walking along the rocky shoreline, wearing that long grey dress she always wore, as well as a grey woollen shawl and a grey lacy bonnet.

"Her feet didn't seem to touch the ground," one of the two men later reported. "It was as if she were supported in mid-air. She just seemed to pull away from us effortlessly no matter how quickly we tried to walk."

"I tried to run after her, but she kept moving away like a cloud drifting across the sky," the other man said. "There were ferns and bushes in her way, but the underbrush didn't move when she passed through it. When she reached the end of the path where the shoreline met the water she looked back in our direction. I couldn't see her face at all. It was as if there was nothing at all beneath that grey lacy bonnet."

Sometimes the Stoney Beach Grey Lady was spotted without a head at all. Her gruesome decapitated spectre is seen, always at a distance and always moving away. Sometimes her ghost stands at the seashore and points out into the water. It's believed that the captain must have cut her head off and thrown it out into the waves, where it was washed away to sea or perhaps just picked over by the bottom-feeding fish.

24: The Grey Lady Of Seaforth

44° 39' 57.26" N, 63° 15' 29.69" W

A NOTHER FAMOUS GREY LADY SIGHTING occurred in the community of Seaforth, about forty minutes outside of Halifax. The community is a thriving shelter for the arts and I know several writers and authors who live out that way. Facing the Atlantic Ocean, near the Chezzetcook Inlet, the village is named for the breathtaking view that the Atlantic graciously supplies.

I have heard two different versions of the story of the Grey Lady of Seaforth.

Darryl Walsh tells one version in his collection *Ghosts of the Atlantic*. In it he talks of how the Grey Lady has been seen floating down the staircase in one particular house in Seaforth. Unfortunately, he only teases the reader with the advice that "if you ask one of the locals nicely enough, they may tell you in which house the Grey Lady can be seen."

That wasn't enough for me so I talked to a few folks and I actually met the owner of the house in which the Grey Lady has been seen. The house is the original rectory of the St. James Anglican Church, located just down the way on the other side of Marine Drive. The Church was established in 1845 and still conducts Sunday services, which are regularly attended by folks whose ancestors were the original parishioners.

The Grey Lady has been seen in that very church rectory. She descends the stairs to the midway point and pauses as if she's heard the door open, perhaps expecting a certain someone to call. When she sees the visitor isn't the one she waits for she stands there, halfway up and halfway down the centre staircase. She never says a word or makes a single sound, and if you put one foot upon that stairway she will vanish, like a startled cat.

A second version of the tale places the Grey Lady outdoors and away from the buildings. Sometimes the Grey Lady stands on the shoreline with the wind blowing her hair behind her like the mane of a galloping horse. Other times the Grey Lady is seen walking through the local graveyard. She always seems to be looking, as if she is either waiting or simply hoping to see a certain someone approaching.

I looked into this story as well. There are two burial grounds situated very close to the church, and locals will tell you that the Grey Lady is often seen walking across the older of the two graveyards. The story that they tell is that the Grey Lady was a woman who lost her husband in a shipwreck and she walks the hills and the shores of Seaforth, waiting for her man to come home from the sea.

I am not going to give you the exact location of the house, because the owner would not appreciate being disturbed by too many visitors, but if you do visit the little community of Seaforth, be sure to do so early in the morning on one of those grey October mornings and you might catch a glimpse of the Grey Lady of Seaforth as she walks her lonely vigil.

25: The Hammering Soldier of Petpeswick

44° 45′ 15.3″ N, 63° 9′ 16.4″ W

I CAME ACROSS THIS STORY FROM three different and unrelated sources that all confirm there is a certain ancient path that rambles through the woodlands that surround the coastal waters of Petpeswick Harbour. The way I see it, this is either a ghost story or the world's scariest knock-knock joke.

"You can hear the sound of hammering, long through the night," one man told me. "My grandmother told me that it was the ghost of a deserter who had been killed while he was attempting to flee from a British troopship that had taken shelter in the harbour."

Let me tell you this story the way I heard it told best.

Hammers, Long Into the Night

As a general rule the coastal waters of Petpeswick Harbour, about twenty-five miles from Halifax, are quiet and calm, but certain local folk say you can hear the soldier's ghost best on nights when the waves roar and pound against the shoreline.

The soldier, whose name was Barnaby, had been a carpenter by trade when he was pressed into service in an Old Portsmouth tavern, after the captain of a press gang bought him a tall tankard of cold ale one hot summer evening.

"Drink up," the captain said. "You look thirsty."

"I am," Barnaby said, and tipped the tankard back.

It was a stupid thing to do but it was a hot night and Barnaby did not have enough money with him to go around turning down free drinks. Besides that, the captain had basically dared him to drink, and Barnaby just could not resist a double-dog-dare. He drank until he felt something cold and metallic touch his lips.

What could it be?

Barnaby reached down into his tankard and fished out a brand new shilling.

And that was how it happened. Just as soon as Barnaby touched that shilling his fate was sealed. You see, back then that was how you joined the British forces. By touching the shilling, Barnaby was automatically enlisted.

It was a dirty trick, and it wasn't quite legal, but there wasn't much Barnaby could do once six strapping press-gang sailors grabbed hold of him and dragged to the ship. Which was how young Barnaby found himself on-board a British troopship, hammering, sawing, and carrying reinforcements for the Halifax Citadel.

One night, an unexpected storm forced the troopship to seek shelter in the harbour.

I bet I could swim to shore, Barnaby thought. I bet I could escape.

He took his chance, running for the ship's railing and vaulting in a single easy leap, taking a deep breath as he arced down into the quiet, deep waters that waited below.

"Man away," an eagle-eyed sailor sang out.

Several sailors aimed muskets from the ship's railing, while others discreetly cheered Barnaby on. Barnaby didn't bother to look back. He swam hard, aiming for the shore. The musket shots splashed about him but he wasn't hit. It is difficult to aim a musket from a rocking boat.

The captain, accompanied by a half of a dozen sailors, lowered a boat and rowed after Barnaby, who by now had reached the shoreline and run for the shelter of the forest.

Then the captain's boat reached the shoreline. The captain calmly raised his musket, took aim, and fired, hitting Barnaby squarely in his back.

The impact pushed Barnaby forward. He threw his arms up into the air as if attempting to surrender, and fell face first in the mud, flopping about like a beached jellyfish.

"Hang him," the captain ordered.

Although Barnaby was clearly dying, the captain was determined to have his vengeance.

The sailors tied a hangman's knot in one end of a rope, wrapping it thirteen times around to ensure a proper kill. Then they threw the other end of the rope up over a thick branch in the nearest tall tree, and looped the noose around Barnaby's neck. The six sailors hand-over-handed Barnaby's body into the air and braced themselves, leaving poor Barnaby hanging and kicking his heels against the trunk of the tree.

Thump, thump, thump, thump ….

"Hold him up there a little while longer," the captain coldly said. "I want to remember this."

Thump, thump, thump, thump ….

Fifteen minutes later, and Barnaby was still kicking.

"Why doesn't he die?" the captain wondered aloud.

"Shall I shoot him again?" one sailor asked.

"Shouldn't we be thinking about burying him?" another sailor suggested.

"Leave him dangle and kick all that he wants," the captain ordered. "The birds can pick his bones."

They tied the free end of the rope onto the trunk of the tree and let poor Barnaby hang up there like a flag of despair. Then they walked back towards the beach and rowed out to the waiting troopship. Only the captain continued to look back at Barnaby, still kicking high above the forest floor.

Thump, thump, thump, thump....

Some will tell you that the captain never survived that night following Barnaby's impromptu execution. Some will tell you that the captain's mind slipped and he died screaming in a London madhouse. Others say that the captain was found in his cabin the next morning, his skull beaten in with a carpenter's hammer.

Some of the older residents of Petpeswick will tell you that on certain cool autumn nights, you can still hear the sound of Barnaby's ghost out in the woods of Petpeswick, kicking and hammering away like a woodpecker gone mad.

Thump, thump, thump, thump....

Is that someone at the door? Maybe you better go and see.

26: The Ghost of Haddon Hall
44° 32' 25" N, 64° 14' 23" W

ABOUT FIFTY MILES WEST OF Halifax on Nova Scotia's south shore is the picturesque little village of Chester. Home to a population of a little over 2,300, Chester is a well-known tourist destination with a colourful history.

For instance, back in the days of the American Revolution, on June 30, 1782, the village of Chester narrowly avoided a raid by the infamous US privateer, Captain Noah Stoddard of Fairhaven, Massachusetts, and four other privateer vessels in a very cinematic and almost unbelievable fashion. The entire population of Chester marched around the village's single piece of fortification, an old unmanned blockhouse, dressed in homemade costumes of red broadcloth. From a distance it looked to the privateers as if there was an entire battalion of British soldiers there, ready for battle. The shipload of privateers thought twice about the whole situation before they beat a hasty retreat out of Chester and just a day later they landed up the coast in the town of Lunenburg, Nova Scotia, and ransacked the entire town.

Now that is a lesson to remember, folks: any time you are faced with adversity, just put on a bold front and brazen it out. You look a whole lot tougher than you might think, no matter what your bathroom mirror tells you.

There are several ghost stories attached to the little town of Chester.

Some folks talk about the midnight wagon and how you can hear the hooves of a ghostly old cart horse clip-clopping along. No one has ever really seen the midnight wagon, you understand. They just hear it creaking and rolling and clip-clopping down the road.

The Visitor Information Centre at 20 Smith Road, formerly the old Chester train station, is also thought to be haunted. The ghost of a little girl has been reported, as well as a mysterious and unexplained shadow that looms upon the wall without any sign of a source at all. The shadow resembles a heavy-set man, stooped with age, wearing a brakeman's cap. Strange creaks and groans can be heard from the upstairs at night and the building has been investigated by a local paranormal team.

Besides the Visitor Information Centre, there is a restaurant known as The Galley, located at 115 Marina Road, a restaurant that was open for many years and was well known for its haunted history. Flashing lights and eerie moans and slamming doors have been witnessed by several paranormal investigators. It is believed that the restaurant was haunted by the spectre of a murder victim. Unfortunately the restaurant is permanently closed, so we may never know the truth behind the ghost of The Galley.

But the most well known ghostly location in the town of Chester is Haddon Hall. The building isn't open to the public anymore but for many decades the hall was *the* place to stay in Chester.

Haddon Hall was built in the Victorian style in 1905. Guests were treated to a spectacular view overlooking the restless waters of Mill Cove. Folks will quite often tell you a story about the ghost of a previous owner by the name of Marie who still haunts this residence. By all reports she is a friendly spirit, only looking to be of help to the folks who live there. However, there is another ghost who has been reported as haunting the fields surrounding Haddon Hall and it is her that I really want to tell you about.

The Ghost of Annie

Her name was Annie and she must have been born on a Wednesday because she was full of woe. She had one of those flat faces, like a pond that has frozen over and refuses to crack. The look in her eyes always made folks think about a cold dreary rainstorm puddling down, and whenever she spoke you kind of had the sinking feeling that she could break into tears at any given point in time.

One of Annie's tricks was to wait in one of the ground-floor rooms of what used to be known as the Gatehouse. Apparently, if a visitor happened to step into that room Annie would slam the door shut and leave that person locked inside. Eventually, the maintenance crew took it upon themselves to break the lock so that the door could not be locked shut.

The story goes that Annie lived in that Gatehouse. She wasn't married but she did have a son. Some people believed that it was the illegitimate son of the gatekeeper while others whispered that it was son of the Lord of the Manor himself.

Annie would never say just who exactly the child's father was.

To make matters worse, the child had been stillborn and Annie never really seemed to get over it. She wrapped herself in a burial shroud and sat in an old rocking chair and just rocked away her day. She sat there in her room, cradling the corpse of the little dead baby, keeping it wrapped in an old quilt that was stained with the residue of death and slow decay.

When authorities tried to take the baby's corpse from her, Annie would resist. She didn't actually physically resist anyone's effort to remove her dead baby from her arms. She didn't hit anyone or try to kick or bite or even use coarse language.

"It was like she sort of froze up and stiffened," one witness stated. "You couldn't move her, no matter how hard you tried. It was like her arms had turned to stone."

After a time the folks just decided to give up on Annie. After all, she wasn't really doing anyone any sort of harm. So they left her to sit and wait there in her rocking chair. They made sure she was fed regularly and she seemed to be able to take care of her other needs and she sat there day in and day out, just rocking away. The gatekeeper and his family could hear that old rocking chair squeaking throughout the whole entire night.

Squeak, squeak, squeak, squeak....

"After a while we just learned to get used to it," the old gatekeeper said. "It was kind of like how you learn to live with mice in your house. After a while you just go about your business and you pay no attention to the squeaking in the walls."

Then one day the squeaking just came to a stop and when the gatekeeper stole out to have a look, poor Annie was leaned back in her rocking chair, stone cold dead. They wrapped her up and carried her out to the field where they buried her.

"It wouldn't do to put her in the church graveyard," the gatekeeper said. "She hadn't been happy with the good Lord and what he had done to her for a very long time. So we dug ourselves a hole and we put her in, dead baby and all."

Since then, witnesses have reported seeing the haunting sight of a woman in a long white gown walking across the grounds surrounding Haddon Hall, her arms cradling a quilted bundle about the size and shape of a baby. Some folks have even tried to catch up to her but they might as well have been trying to catch hold of a vagrant midnight breeze.

27: Mahone Bay and the Ghost of the *Young Teazer*

44° 30′ 0″ N, 64° 13′ 0″ W

T HE PRIVATEER SCHOONER KNOWN AS the *Young Teazer* left Portland, Maine, on the morning of June 3, 1813. She had a crew of seventy-three sailors, eager to board enemy merchantmen. That was just exactly what a privateer did for a living. A privateer was basically an honest-to-shiver-me-timbers pirate with a license to steal—a charter granted to them by whichever government they happened to be serving. The privateers earned their pay by capturing enemy ships and selling them to the highest bidder.

Now, the *Young Teazer* was a very special sort of a ship. She was a two-masted schooner constructed specifically for privateering. Built of Norwegian pine and American oak, and lined with cork in order to protect the crew from flying splinters should the ship happen to be hit with a cannon blast.

The captain of the *Young Teazer* was William D. Dobson. Serving as the ship's second-in-command was Lieutenant Frederick Johnson.

Things started out well, as the *Young Teazer* captured two British merchant vessels just off of the Sambro Island Lighthouse. When the *Young Teazer* was pursued by a British vessel, the frigate HMS *Orpheus,* Captain Dobson had the crew run up a British flag that he had kept for just such an occasion. The British were completely fooled by his ruse but only for a short time.

A while later, the British caught up with the *Young Teazer* after an eighteen-hour chase, cornering her just outside of Mahone Bay. And that was where it all went down.

The British vessel in question was the HMS *Hogue,* a massive seventy-four-cannon ship of the line, a regular schoolyard bully. With only five cannons at her command—or eight if you count the three dummy wooden guns, which were only built to fool unwary merchantmen—the *Young Teazer* was completely outgunned.

Mind you, the little schooner was a lot more maneuverable than the massive *Hogue,* but that only bought the *Young Teazer* a very little bit of breathing space. To make matters worse, the British frigate HMS *Orpheus* arrived to further stack the odds against the American vessel.

Lieutenant Frederick Johnson knew that sooner or later the ship of the line was going to come within firing range of the *Young Teazer* and blow her out of the water. As far as the captain of the HMS *Hogue* saw the whole matter, the *Young Teazer* only had two choices: fight or die.

To make matters worse, the British lowered five dories full of troops who began rowing towards the *Young Teazer.* There was to be no escape. The *Young Teazer* was completely surrounded; however, Lieutenant Frederick Johnson had other ideas.

He absolutely did not want to be caught by the British forces.

The sad truth was that the *Young Teazer* had already been caught once before by the British forces, and the crew had been forced to sign a parole statement solemnly swearing that they would not wage war of any sort against the British Navy—which meant that because they *were* waging war, they would most likely be hanged for breaking their parole.

"Let us set fire to the whole ship," Lieutenant Johnson commanded. "The British will pull back, for fear of the fire. Then, in the ensuing confusion, we can make for the safety of the shore in a lifeboat of our own."

It was too bad that Lieutenant Johnson forgot about the extra barrels of gunpowder he had ordered loaded aboard the ship before they left port. As a result, just as soon as his men had obeyed his command to set fire to the ship, a stray spark reached one of the powder kegs and the ship went up like a floating volcano. Trees shook and window panes were broken and sparks rained down upon nearby Mahone Bay.

Approximately thirty out of the crew of thirty-eight were killed in the blast. The water was littered with pieces of the *Young Teazer,* including her alligator figurehead, and the bones of that brave little vessel washed up on the shoreline for weeks afterwards.

Several of the survivors were also saved from capture. Pieces of the decimated vessel were salvaged and resurrected into various useful purposes. Several large timbers were used in the construction of the well-known Chester restaurant, The Rope Loft. A piece of the ship's keel was fashioned into a heavy and authoritative-looking cross that can be seen in St. Stephen's Anglican Church, also located in Chester.

I have also heard from another storyteller that a piece taken from the captain's cabin was carved into a holy reredos—that is, the large ornate screen placed behind the altar of a church. Apparently one of the former priests of the church in question felt the wood the reredos had been carved from was cursed. The priest had the screen removed and burned, and scattered its ashes in the harbour.

I have also heard that the bodies that had been washed ashore were buried outside of the graveyard fence in unmarked graves, so there is a very good chance—assuming one believes in the supernatural forces that surround an unmarked grave—that the spirits of these dead sailors still walk the night around that church.

Since then there have been many reported sightings of the *Young Teazer* on the waters of Mahone Bay. People see the ghostly vessel sailing through the harbour. Some claim to have heard the doomed sailors screaming from the decks. They say they have heard the crackling of the flames and the creaking of the ropes in the running blocks.

Whether there is a ghost ship out there or not, the people of Mahone Bay still celebrate the memory of the *Young Teazer* faithfully every year. Some years they even send a small replica of the *Young Teazer* out into the harbour's water.

Only don't take my word for it. Go on and make a visit to Mahone Bay some summer and see if you can catch a glimpse of the ghost ship for yourself.

28: The Moser River Mauler

44°58′03″N 62°15′39″W

MOSER RIVER, A SMALL COMMUNITY located on Highway 7 running along the Atlantic Ocean coastline about 141 kilometres east of Halifax, on the head of the Necum Teuch Harbour, is home to a very eerie beast no one has ever seen, but a whole lot of folks have heard.

Moser River was established in 1783 as a way station and a lumber town. The town—and the river that flows beside the town—were named after Henry Moser of Lunenburg, who settled in the area along with his wife, Johanna. You can still see his gravestone standing at Early Settlers Cemetery, which is located on wooded private property at the end of Hannah Lane. A lot of locals don't even know this cemetery is out there; it is difficult to find. However, you can see it quite clearly from the ocean if you happen to be sailing by.

The bulk of Moser River's economy was built upon the three-legged milk stool of fishing, forestry, and tourism. The locals have grown used to a seasonal existence, and have time to indulge themselves in the fine old art of storytelling. I came across this story in bits and pieces—from an early newspaper article, an old folklore magazine, and a long-out-of-print story collection. Nobody really seems to agree upon the facts behind this particular story. All most people remember is there is something making a lot of noise out in the darkness of the deep forest that surrounds the Moser River area.

There is Something Moving Out There in the Bushes

Let me take you back to the year 1900. A young man by the name of Harold MacNamara was preparing to head home after a wild kitchen party at his neighbour's house. The sky had clouded up and it started to rain.

"You ought to stay the night," the neighbour suggested. "I wouldn't want you to catch your death of cold."

"There's no need to worry," Harold replied. "I could find my way home from here wearing a blindfold."

Walking home in the dark back then wasn't easy: there were very few roads, no streetlights, and the path he walked upon wasn't anything more than a grim prayer through the Moser River woods. Halfway home, Harold began to regret his hasty decision to leave. Then he heard a heavy rustling sound, coming at him through the woods.

There was something moving out there in the bushes. It could have been a rabbit. It could have been a skunk. It could have been the wind in the trees. But Harold knew it made too much noise to be anything less than a full-grown bear. Nova Scotia black bears aren't usually much trouble—unless it's a mother bear and you get between her and her cubs—but there's no way of knowing what it might do.

Harold raised his arms above his head and roared loudly in an attempt to frighten the bear away. His father had tried this one before on a bear that he had stumbled across, but that was in broad daylight and the bear had been happy to head in another direction. Somehow, Harold felt a whole lot less confident trying this particular manoeuver in the dark.

What happened next scared Harold MacNamara out of about twenty-three-and-a-half years of breathing. The beast shrieked loudly enough to crack three of Harold MacNamara's front teeth; it sounded something like a cross between a screech owl, a red fox, and a bobcat.

The bushes parted as the beast pushed forward. Harold's knees buckled. He leaned backwards trying to scramble out of reach of whatever was making so much noise, before falling flat onto the bony parts of his chair-polishing muscles, which hurt a lot.

The beast-creature continued its advance, or at least Harold guessed it was still advancing. It was hard to tell in the darkness. He could see the bushes parting as if something large, heavy, and hungry was steadily pushing through the bushes towards him, only he could not see a thing at all.

Harold sensed the bushes parting. He watched as a set of large, reptilian footprints form upon the frosty forest floor in front of him, as if the footprints were forming themselves. The beast was completely invisible. Harold dragged himself backward. The invisible beast continued to squall as it advanced upon him.

Then Harold pushed hard against the frozen dirt, scrambling awkwardly to his feet. He stepped backward, trying not to trip. Finally, he found the strength to turn and run, almost running face-first into an ancient pine tree. He thought briefly about climbing the tree to safety, but there was no guarantee the beast wouldn't climb up after him.

Besides that, it might just stay under the tree and keep Harold up there until morning. The odds were Harold would freeze to death or fall out of the tree into the invisible jaws of the beast below. So Harold stepped around the tree and ran, praying his feet knew more about direction than his head did.

He kept on running. He nearly brained himself silly against a half dozen trees that seemed to almost jump out in front of him when he was busy frantically looking over his shoulder at the beast-creature thing he still could not see—and once he almost ran straight into the depths of the Moser River itself.

By now the beast was a whole lot closer. Harold smelled its breath, and felt the beast was just about to take a bite out his cowlick down to his ears. He ran all the faster, his breath burning inside of his lungs.

Finally Harold reached the door of his home. He nearly broke his key off in the lock, but the door suddenly swung open and his mother, Mary MacNamara, stood there reciting the Lord's Prayer at the top of her lungs.

"Close the door," Harold shouted, only when he looked back all sign of the beast had vanished.

"What is it?" his mother asked.

"You ought to know," Harold said. "It was your praying that scared it off."

Harold's mother looked oddly puzzled.

"Was it really my praying that did it?" she asked.

"I can't think of any other reason for it to have backed away from the door like it did," Harold said. "It was a bad evil spirit, and your holy prayers frightened it away. How did you know what to do? Did you see that beast-creature coming through the woods?"

"I didn't see a blessed thing," Harold's mother said, shaking her head. "I was praying for your soul, you coming home so late at night, worrying your mother like you did. I was warming up with the Lord's Prayer, and was fixing to slip half a dozen Hail Mary's into the mix before finishing off with a recitation of the entire Sermon on the Mount, just to try and teach you a lesson about coming home too late at night."

Which only goes to show that you should never mess with a momma bear of any kind. Nothing is fiercer than a Nova Scotia momma.

SECTION 5
Central & Halifax

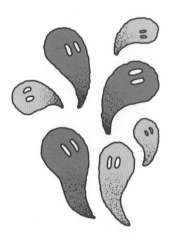

28: Where the Ghost Walks

44.5054° N, 63.6630° W

WHENEVER I TALK ABOUT THE ghosts of the city of Halifax I invariably find myself drawn to the shores of Georges Island.

It is funny, but Georges Island is one of the few haunted locations in Halifax I have never actually been to. The island is only open certain days of the year, and you generally have to pay admission to go there and that kind of holds me back just a little bit.

That's right, folks. You heard it here first: Steve Vernon is a cheap old son of a bear.

I believe that Georges Island comes to my mind first because it is the first place that both the French and British forces first set foot.

Let me tell you a bit about the island's history.

The island is a drumlin—a mound of hard-packed gravel,

sand, silt, and clay—much like the other famous Halifax drumlin that would eventually come to be known as Citadel Hill. It was a natural spot for a landing force because you could land and set up a base camp on Georges Island and so long as you kept careful watch there was no way an opposing force could sneak up on you. The island was small enough so that you could easily keep an eye in all directions. The only way an enemy could approach you would be by canoe or by boat and such a force would be all too easily spotted.

Back in the late 1600s the island was known as *Île à la Raquette* which is French for Snowshoe Island. It was named after the small oval snowshoes sometimes known as bear paws that were favoured by the local Mi'kmaq. In fact, back in the late seventeenth century, the island was actually occupied by an Acadian family of three (husband, wife, and son) as well as a small settlement of Mi'kmaq consisting of seven men, seven women, and nineteen children. By all reports the two micro-communities got along famously.

In the summer of 1746, King Louis XV ordered a huge fleet of sixty-four warships and eleven thousand men to sail from France to set up base in Halifax Harbour. The plan was for this military force to retake Port Royal (Annapolis Royal) from the British, as well as the famous Fortress of Louisbourg that had fallen the year before. In fact, King Louis XV had the generally hopeful idea that the force could push the British completely out of Nova Scotia.

The force was led by the famed French Admiral Jean-Baptiste Louis Frédéric de La Rochefoucauld de Roye, otherwise known as the Duc d'Anville. Unfortunately, the voyage from France was totally ill-starred. Storms and blasts of lightning and talk of mutiny and bouts of scurvy, typhus, and fever took a toll on both the numbers of the French force as well as their general morale. It has been estimated that as many as two thousand men died during the ill-fated voyage.

On September 10, 1746, the remainder of the French invasion fleet woefully limped into Halifax Harbour and set up a base camp and field hospital upon the island that was formerly known as the *Île à la Raquette,* which the Duc d'Anville promptly and immodestly renamed as the *Île d'Enville.*

Six days later, the Duc d'Anville keeled over with what was then known as an apoplectic seizure, although a modern-day doctor would be able to tell you the condition is now better known as a hemorrhagic stroke resulting from the rupture of a blood vessel.

Following his death, a small work party was sworn to secrecy and the Duc d'Anville's remains were buried in a secret location upon the island known as the *Île d'Enville.* The burial was secret, because it was feared that certain disgruntled members of his forces might decide to dig up the Duc d'Anville's remains out of pure hateful spite.

However, before the burial commenced the surgeon decided to remove Duc D'Anville's heart from his chest. The organ was placed in a biscuit tin, which was then filled with hot wax in order to prevent the organ's decay. The biscuit tin was eventually returned to France and presented to Duc d'Anville's widow and three children.

Shortly afterwards the entire invasion fleet turned back around and returned to France and folks forgot all about the change in the island's name until the year 1749 when the island was renamed George Island, in honour of King George II. Then, in the year 1963, the island was renamed Georges Island.

Over the years since that would-be invasion fleet first landed, the ghost of Duc d'Anville has been sighted walking from the island, straight across the harbour and into downtown Halifax. Sometimes he walks across the water and other times he walks along the shore. He has also been seen walking up Duke Street towards Citadel Hill.

In addition to the walking ghost of Duc d'Anville, there have been several reported sightings of one of his warships—its sails flapping and a skeleton crew working on deck.

One wonders what the old gentleman Duc d'Anville must

think of this city, especially since he actually died before a single Halifax building was ever built.

The Other Ghosts of Georges Island

In addition to the ghost of Duc d'Anville, there have been many other sightings reported, although none of them had any actual names attached. There have been stories of the dead rising up from the unmarked graves upon Georges Island—and although there was never an actual cemetery upon the island, it has been home to many darker pieces of Haligonian history.

In 1751 a pair of run-down storage sheds were converted into Halifax's very first jailhouse, known appropriately enough as His Majesty's Gaol. The cells were small and dark and cold and damp and would have been more appropriate for the storage of potatoes and various other roots, rather than local Halifax criminals, traitors, pirates, mutineers, and assorted deserters.

Floggings and hangings were common occurrences. Stories were often told of people looking out over the harbour on certain nights and seeing the ghosts of hanged men dangling over the tiny island.

Then, from 1755 to 1763, the facilities were expanded to allow room for approximately nine hundred French prisoners, primarily captured off of the coast of Louisbourg. Just take a good look at that little island out there and try and imagine it serving as a home to that many military prisoners.

Perhaps this is the origin behind the sighting of a one-armed aged French officer who is often spotted upon the southwest corner of the island, gazing wistfully towards the mouth of the harbour.

Amazingly enough, a year or two later even more room was made for the imprisonment of thousands of Acadians during the Expulsion. The authorities forced thousands of Acadians onto the shores of Georges Island during the Expulsion. They were made to camp out in the open, huddled around small campfires and cooking pots, even in the heart of winter. The lucky ones found temporary shelter thanks to the construction of a couple of more barracks. Hundreds died on the beaches of that small island.

Following the end of the Expulsion, Georges Island was put to use as a quarantine station for ship crews suspected of suffering from an assortment of communicable diseases such as yellow fever, small pox, cholera, and the like.

Then, in the spring of 1776, the first King's Naval Hospital was constructed on Georges Island, putting some of the remaining facilities left over from the quarantine station to good use.

It was around this time that folks began reporting another Woman in Grey, only this time her grey gown was always sopping wet and tangled with seaweed. Some believed that she had swum ashore from a sunken ship and had spent her last hours waiting on the shoreline for her one true love to swim ashore. And then, when she realized that her lover hadn't made it to the shore, she swam back out into the water and drowned.

So, with all the disease and death and tragedy and suffering that has surrounded this little island throughout the combination of quarantines and disease, crime and punishment, and the outright expulsion of anywhere from twelve to fifteen thousand Acadians, there is an awful lot of room for suffering and tragedy: the building blocks of any good ghost story.

30: The Ghost of Alexander Keith

44°38'30.80"N, 63°34'11.01"W

ALEXANDER KEITH FIRST PURCHASED THIS building back in 1821. Keith established his very own brewery on the property, brewing many beverages under his name, including strong ale, porter, ginger wine, table beer, and spruce beers. In 1837, he decided to upgrade the location and built the current ironstone brewery, making it one of the more finely constructed buildings in the Hollis Street area.

His timing was perfect. Due partly to the 1833 abolition of slavery in the West Indies which caused a drastic slowdown in the sugar trade—which in turn triggered a further slowdown in the rum trade—people began to drink beer. Keith's beer.

Since Alexander Keith passed away on December 14, 1873, folks have continued to report hearing his calm and measured footsteps in a certain tunnel that led between his brewery and his home. Sometimes he is heard to be running.

Why is he running? I don't really know. Perhaps there is a midnight beer emergency.

Far more disturbing is the fact that several maintenance workers at the brewery have also reported witnessing the image of a screaming man, his face streaming with blood, whose nightmarish visage has been seen staring out of a certain mirror in a certain men's washroom, located in one of the lower floors of the building.

Alexander Keith's remains were buried at Camp Hill Cemetery, roughly in the middle of the property. On Keith's birthday, October 5, locals and tourists alike visit his grave and leave either a Keith's beer bottle or else a simple beer cap to commemorate the gentleman.

31: The Privateer's Warehouse

44° 39' 3.8520" N 63° 34' 57.6732" W

LET'S START OUT WITH A definition of what exactly a privateer is. Basically, a privateer is a bit like a pirate, only with a government-supplied license. Another way to look at is that the difference between a pirate and a privateer is kind of like the difference between a poacher and a hunter. A hunter has a rifle and a license and a poacher has a rifle as well—and he is just hoping that he does not get caught.

Built back in 1790, The Privateer's Warehouse is one of the oldest and most-storied buildings that stand upon the Halifax waterfront. It was also the headquarters of one of the canniest businessmen in eighteenth-century Halifax—Enos Collins. (Kindly do not snicker over the man's first name. It was common enough back then.)

Enos Collins made himself an awful lot of money funding one of the most successful privateer vessels that ever set sail during the War of 1812. The vessel was known as the *Liverpool Packet*, and captured fifty American vessels during a brief wartime career that spanned just a little less than two years.

The Many Lives of the Liverpool Packet

The *Liverpool Packet* started out her life as an American slave ship, sailing under the name *Severn*. The *Severn* was a clipper ship, weighing in at about sixty-seven tons and built for speed. She was captured by a British sixteen-gun sloop, the HMS *Tartarus,* just off of the West African coastline while she was tending a Spanish slave ship. The *Tartarus* escorted the *Severn* across the Atlantic Ocean to Halifax Harbour, where it was ordered that the *Severn* be sold at auction as an illegal slave ship.

The *Severn* had not been cared for, and was given the rather unflattering nickname of *The Black Joke*, in reference to her career in illegal slavery. Yet, beneath all of the grime, shame, and utter misuse, she was still a prime vessel. Her masts were raked at a slight angle and even standing still moored at the Halifax dock, she looked as if she were ready to run.

Enos Collins bought the *Severn* for a slightly-out-of-tune song. Then he fumigated the reek of human captivity out of her with a strong and smoking mixture of sulphur, vinegar, and black tar. He armed her with one six-pounder cannon and four larger twelve-pounder cannons he had purchased second-hand. The cannons had been serving as fence posts on a waterfront property. He crewed her with a full complement of forty sailors and set her loose on the open sea, operating under the name of the *Liverpool Packet*.

For those folks who want to know, a packet ship was simply a ship that delivered packets of mail. The *Liverpool Packet* was built for speed, and Enos Collins's choice of vessel made perfect sense.

However, Collins had other plans. He knew that there was a war coming soon, and he had all of the necessary paperwork ready to secure a license for privateering, waiting for the moment war was officially proclaimed. He knew he would stand to make a whole lot more profit out of privateering than out of postal delivery.

(Maybe Canada Post ought to think about opening a sideline pirate business to make up for all of the business email has taken from them.)

The *Liverpool Packet's* initial run at privateering was happily successful, as she ambushed a total of thirty-three American merchant ships off of Cape Cod and sending them straight on back to Nova Scotia manned by a skeleton crew. Sadly, however, the *Liverpool Packet* was chased down and captured on June 10, 1813.

Once captured, the *Liverpool Packet* sailed under American command, renamed *The Young Teaser's Ghost* in honour of the American privateer *Young Teazer*.

Yup, that would be the very same *Young Teazer* that blew itself up and now haunts the coastal waters of Mahone Bay. I am not sure just why the new owners decided to change the "z" in *Young Teazer* to an "s" in *The Young Teaser's Ghost*. I guess spelling has always been a mystery to most folks.

Unfortunately, *The Young Teaser's Ghost* had very little luck as a privateer and failed to capture a single British vessel. She was repurchased by another American entrepreneur and renamed the *Portsmouth Packet*. The new name and the new captain brought her no better luck. As the *Portsmouth Packet* she *still* could not catch a single British vessel.

She did manage to get herself chased down by the British eighteen-gun brig-sloop, HMS *Fantome*, assisted by a similarly sized brig-sloop known as the HMS *Epervier*. A brig-sloop usually ran about 380 tons. They were built stout and fast and the little clipper now known as the *Portsmouth Packet* did not stand a chance against them. The two British brig-sloops chased her down after a thirteen-hour run and escorted her to Halifax, where Enos Collins once again purchased her and gave her a fresh new crew.

So, are you keeping up here?

We have gone from the *Severn* to the *Liverpool Packet* to *The Young Teaser's Ghost* to the *Portsmouth Packet*—four different names for the very same ship. Back then, ships were traded like used cars are today.

So, Enos Collins bought the freshly captured *Portsmouth Packet* and gave her back her original name of the *Liverpool Packet*. Over the summer of 1814 she captured fourteen more American prizes. Her very last capture was the forty-ton American schooner *The Fair Trader*. Depending upon the source material, the *Liverpool Packet* captured anywhere from fifty to one hundred to two hundred enemy vessels, some of which were released, some lost, and some recaptured by the Americans—for a total value of up to $1 million, which was one of the reasons that Enos Collins was the richest man in Nova Scotia.

For the bit of money that he paid in the beginning, Enos Collins earned himself a tidy profit. Eventually, after the war ended and privateering was once again declared illegal, Enos Collins sold the *Liverpool Packet* to an undisclosed buyer.

The little ship that kicked the heck out of the American navy vanished, just like a ghost, from the pages of history just as easily as she first appeared there.

The Ghost of Privateer's Warehouse

In the early 1970s, this cluster of stone and wooden warehouses was rescued from the wrecking ball, thanks to a proclamation designating it a National Historic Site. Three city blocks worth of buildings, built back in the late 1700s to the early 1800s, still stand today as a must-see location for any visitors to Halifax.

Mind you, it is a lot quieter there these days then it was when I first came to Halifax about forty years ago. Back then, Historic Properties was a destination and it was always crowded. Nowadays, things have changed. Time will do that to anything that you can think of.

The ghost of Enos Collins has been seen lingering in the shadows of the Historic Properties, particularly in the lower offices of the Privateers Warehouse. Employees have reported seeing a ghostly shadow moving through the hallways and staircases. Footsteps have been heard echoing through the darkened corridors. Some employees have even refused to work after the sun has gone down.

Perhaps the ghost of Enos Collins is still lingering on, in the hopes of closing one more big deal. Perhaps he is waiting for the third return of the *Liverpool Packet*. Whatever the reason his ghost still lingers in these two-hundred-year-old buildings, I certainly would not want to stay overnight to see if he shows up.

32: A Triple-Barrelled Curse
44.6637°N 63.5846°W

ONE OF HALIFAX'S MOST FAMOUS paranormal legends concerns the curse that is supposed to have been laid upon the Angus L. Macdonald Bridge, which stretches across the passage of water known as the Narrows.

The story here is a tale of fierce love and cold betrayal and an act of vengeance that is both sudden and far-reaching. It is also one of the first stories I ever heard told about Halifax when I first arrived in this fine city.

A British sailor worked his way into a Mi'kmaw maiden's heart and he persuaded her to run away with him, even though she was already promised to another man.

She lived in a settlement in Tufts Cove. You will see this area while you are driving or walking across the bridge. The settlement would have been located where those three gigantic candy-cane-striped smokestacks are standing. That settlement is no longer, of course. It was completely destroyed by the Halifax Explosion.

"I have a dory by the shoreline," the sailor told her. "We can row to my ship and be happy together."

I do not think that this sailor meant everything that he said. It is quite possible, mind you, that he spoke the truth. Perhaps he truly loved this girl, yet I somehow think that no matter what he said to her and what she did in return, sooner or later it would have ended in tears.

Which was how it turned out, after all.

The sailor and the maiden left her village and made their way down to the shoreline but they were not alone. Her promised love, a young and powerful warrior, angered by her betrayal, followed them down to the shoreline and came at them with a raised hatchet.

Now some storytellers will tell you that he meant to strike her with his hatchet and others will tell you that he was aiming for the sailor and she threw herself in between the angry hatchet and her one true love. Either way, the maiden was struck down dead by one single powerful blow of the warrior's hatchet.

In the ensuing confusion, the sailor managed to clamber into the dory and push it out to sea. He began to row for his ship, not bothering to look behind him. He did not even bother to look and see if the maiden had lived.

The warrior waded out into the water and began to swim in an attempt to catch up with the sailor in the dory, but the waters were rough and the sailor was an experienced oarsmen and he already had a lead on the warrior.

Or perhaps the warrior simply lost heart in his grief over his fallen love.

In either case, the warrior swam as far as he could manage before sinking into the deep and unforgiving depths of Tufts Cove.

The warrior's ancient father, who, depending on who is telling the story, was either a Mi'kmaw chief or else a mighty man of powerful magic, arrived too late to save his son. He could only stand there at the shoreline, staring out at the white man in the dory rowing away towards the safety of his ship.

He knew that there was nothing to be done about it, but he did something all the same.

"FIRST IN A STORM," the old man howled out. "SECOND IN SILENCE, AND THIRD IN DEATH!"

His words boomed and echoed across the waves like a roll of ominous thunder. He was speaking Mi'kmaw and I do not know who thought to write these words down and translate them, but this is what they say the old man said.

It is believed the man's words were both a prophecy and a curse that would signal the fall of a bridge that had not even been built yet. In any case, there would be three bridges built across that stretch of water.

The first bridge, a long fish-hooked railroad trestle, fell on September 7, 1891, during a powerful and unexpected rainstorm.

The second bridge, hastily rebuilt upon the wreckage of the first, fell two years later on the morning of July 24, 1893. The main reason it fell was it had been poorly secured—or rather, not secured at all—to the original bridge's base support. It fell in total silence. Those who saw it fall say it just slid down like a mountain drift of melting snow.

The third bridge is the one that stands today, and some people still wonder if the old man's curse is destined to come true.

You might laugh, but city council actually felt strongly enough about this curse that they consulted a one-hundred-year-old Mi'kmaw Elder before the bridge was opened to the public. On the day of the bridge's opening on November 16, 1945, a small band of Mi'kmaw Elders danced across the bridge, singing a sacred song to ensure the curse of the Macdonald Bridge would be finally broken.

Which is all well and good, but if it is all the same to you I will take the ferry across the Narrows and leave that bridge alone.

33: A Fortress Built on the Bones of a Double Dozen Ghost Stories

44° 38′ 51″ N, 63° 34′ 49″ W

I F HALIFAX IS INDEED THE heart of Nova Scotia, then the Halifax Citadel is the very heart of Halifax itself. Just stand there on the waterfront and look in at the city and you just can't miss it. Citadel Hill just sort of roars up and looms down over the city like a gigantic Steven Spielberg movie backdrop.

Besides that, Citadel Hill holds the very unique distinction of being—in my opinion—the single-most haunted location in all of Nova Scotia. Heck, it even has its very own ghost tour!

However, the hill you are looking at used to be a fair bit higher. Back in 1749, when the British expeditionary force landed with thirteen transport ships and a military sloop of war to begin constructing what would eventually become known as the city of Halifax, the hill that it would stand upon was approximately thirty metres higher than it stands today.

From the very beginning, Halifax was seen by Britain to be a naval and military bastion against the French, who had been tug-of-warring with Britain for the whole of North America for many years prior to that. Mind you, nobody bothered to ask the thousands of local Mi'kmaq, who had been living in Nova Scotia for a measly ten thousand years or so.

One of the first things built was a wooden fort high upon the glacial drumlin that is Citadel Hill. On both sides of that wooden fort a very large wall was constructed to encircle the entire settlement. Both fort and wall were built from the very tall trees that were felled during the clearing of the city. That modest wooden fort was the very first version of the Citadel.

In 1761, the British military engineer Major General John Henry Bastide tore down the old fort, which by this time was practically falling down of its own accord. He constructed a maze of protective earthworks—which required an awful lot of earth. In order to supply the necessary earth, as well as to fashion a solid flat base for the new blockhouse to be erected upon, the hill was cut down by approximately forty feet.

Unfortunately, although the construction crew did a fine job of building the blockhouse, the earthwork defence system was thrown up; pretty much built without a plan in mind. In fact, the kindest description would be to say the earthworks were a full-scale mess. In time the structure gradually decayed and it wasn't until 1793 that a third Halifax Citadel was constructed under the careful eye of Prince Edward, the Duke of Kent.

Prince Edward built the star-shaped fortress that stands there today. The distinctive star shape was tactically superior to the old wooden blockhouse. No matter what direction an enemy advanced on the fortress, the defenders could rain down a killing barrage from three separate directions.

However, Prince Edward was compelled to tear down the old wooden blockhouse and to further level the hill by another fifteen feet. As a result, the construction wasn't completed until 1856.

It might surprise you to discover that the 150-metre-high glacial drumlin Fort George stands upon is actually about 55 feet shorter than it was when the British first decided to build the city of Halifax. If you add in the height of an average fully grown tree, which is what Citadel Hill was covered with before the British got busy with their axes, you will see what was there in a 1749 is a heck of a lot shorter than what is there now.

That's right: Citadel Hill has shrunk.

The Grey Lady of the Cavalier Building
Only you didn't want to read about a boring old history lesson, now did you? You wanted to hear about the ghosts of Citadel Hill. Let's start off by telling you about the Sergeant's Lady—or, as some people call her, the Grey Lady of the Cavalier Building.

I'm going to pretend you just paid the entrance fee for Fort George and you're taking a good long look around. It's likely you're looking at the Cavalier Building, directly across from the entrance. It's the biggest and fanciest building in the entire fort, with rows of wide shiny windows, and a double-decker colonnaded porch.

The building was constructed to serve as the main quarters for officers and many of the soldiers garrisoned there. The building also served as a keep—which is a term for a last-stand kind of a structure. Just picture the enemy storming Citadel Hill, breaking their way through the gates. At this point the commanding officer would give the word to retire to the keep. The soldiers would take cover inside the Cavalier Building, most likely lining up along that big double-decker porch, resting their long muskets on the railing, and firing as fast as possible on the enemy below. Perhaps they paused every now and then to look at each other nervously, trying not to look as if they were thinking to themselves that this whole thing wasn't going to end well.

Which it wouldn't.

Mind you, the soldiers who served in the Citadel never had to face that situation.

That's right. Believe it or not, in the whole entire two-hundred-and-fifty-odd-year lifespan of the Citadel Fortress, there has *never* been a single shot fired in anger—unless you count the musket blasts that missed the target when the soldiers were engaged in target practice down on the grassy area we now call Wanderer's Grounds.

But Death has darkened these Citadel walls, and that brings us to this first story.

Up on the second floor, people have seen the ghost of a young woman, all dressed in grey. She sits and rocks on an ancient willow rocking chair. It's believed she is the ghost of a sergeant's wife. It seems the lonely lady died in a fire that apparently took place in the Citadel Barracks in the Cavalier Building in the summer of 1889. She was caught in the smoke and choked to death.

Mind you, sometimes you do not see her. Sometimes all you see is that grey willow rocking chair, tipping back and forth—and as any grandmother who knows her Maritime folklore can tell you, a rocking chair rocking by itself is a sure sign of impending Death.

Other folks claim to have heard that rocking chair, squeaking and creaking against the painted pine floorboards. They didn't see the chair, you understand. They just heard the sound of the grey lady rocking the lonely centuries away, as steadily as the waves washing upon the Halifax shoreline.

There have been one or two sightings from the night watchmen who keep an eye on the building after the visitors have all gone home. They will tell you that they did not actually see a ghost, but they could see the flicker of a lantern, again up on the second floor of the Cavalier Building's upper veranda.

Other witnesses have caught sight of a nameless Canadian Army private in a Second World War drab khaki uniform, seen to be standing upon the second-floor veranda of the Cavalier Building. If you try and approach this lonely figure, he will turn and walk away from you and then step straight into the wall.

Ghosts do that sometimes.

I am afraid I haven't heard much in the way of a story behind this First World War apparition, but it's a fact that the Citadel facilities were used to provide temporary barracks for the soldiers waiting to be shipped to Europe as well as serving as the central coordinating headquarters for the city's anti-aircraft defenses.

The very last reported apparition in the Cavalier Building has only been heard, rather than seen. Witnesses swear you can hear the sound of his footsteps steadily climbing up to the second-floor veranda of the Cavalier Building, apparently visiting the Grey Lady at her rocking chair. Some folks claim to have glimpsed him out of the corner of their eye, but no reliable description has ever been ventured. He is nothing more than a lonely echo from the distant past.

But the Grey Lady of the Cavalier Building and her mysterious followers aren't the only ghosts reported to haunt the Halifax Citadel.

The Clock Tower Ghost

Depending upon who you talk to, the guides at the Citadel will tell you there is a second lonely grey lady who keeps a solitary vigil at the base of the Citadel Hill clock tower.

You'll see her best on foggy autumn nights, when the wind blows across the grassy undulations of Citadel Hill. A long-time member of the Citadel's 78th Highlanders who gave me a personal tour of the facilities told me about her.

"Not many know of her," he told me. "And not many have seen her, but once you've seen her you'll never forget the sight of her. Her eyes will sing out to you and I'm certain that on my deathbed I will look up and remember that fateful moonlit night when I saw her standing beside the clock tower."

Some sources speak of a soldier who was engaged to a woman by the name of Cassie Allen. It seems Cassie had promised to marry this soldier but the night before the wedding an ex-suitor told Cassie the soldier was already married to a woman who had lost her mind and was in a Bermuda asylum.

"The fever took her mind," the jealous ex-suitor told Cassie. "He won't own up to her. I wouldn't marry a man like that, if I were you."

When the fiancé heard of this slanderous gossip a fistfight broke out between him and the ex-suitor. In the confusion he broke the neck of the ex-suitor who was better at spreading gossip than defending himself. Facing an impending court martial and a long and possibly fatal term in a military prison, not to mention the loss of Cassie's love, the fiancé hanged himself. They say to this day that the spirit of Cassie keeps a lonely midnight watch for her long-lost love.

I'm not certain if the clock tower ghost has any sort of relation to the grey lady of the Cavalier Building, but I have a feeling the two of them have some sort of bone to pick.

Company on the Tour

There are tours given every single day of the summer through the Citadel and I definitely recommend you take at least one trip through the majestic old fortress, but I ought to warn you about one certain phenomenon: it seems there is the ghost of a very young girl who accompanies the tours in a strange and particular fashion.

Many tour-goers over the years have reported the odd sensation of a young child's hand clasping their own as they walk through the darkened halls of certain areas of the Citadel.

"She squeezed my hand whenever I got scared," one tour-goer reported. "I'm not sure who was more frightened, her or me."

So be careful what you reach for. It might grab you right back.

The Sergeant's Ghost of Casement 18

Lastly, one of the nastiest and most gruesome ghosts people have seen lurking and stomping and swearing within the walls of the Halifax Citadel is the one-armed colour-sergeant's ghost.

Let me tell you a little bit about that fellow.

The colour-sergeant was reported to be a bit of a bully. Now, that can come with the job a Sergeant has to do: relaying the orders of his superiors to the men in the ranks, and then making sure the soldiers carry those orders out. You become accustomed to being obeyed without a question.

However, this particular colour-sergeant seemed to really enjoy pushing people around, and there is a great deal of difference between being a man of authority as opposed to someone who is just a plain old-fashioned bully.

Well, it seems this particular colour-sergeant disappeared on the very same night of the summer barracks fire. It was believed he had simply deserted in the confusion, and most folks agreed it was simply a case of good riddance to bad rubbish.

However, later that winter the water began to taste awfully funky and peculiar—or, at least a whole lot more funky and peculiar than usual, it being the nineteenth century.

I should tell you a bit about that well. It isn't the sort of well you might envision. There isn't a picturesque stone wall with a tastefully shingled roof and a quaint little bucket suspended over it. Rather, this well was hidden inside the building, behind a door marked CASEMENT 18. You see, it was necessary to keep the well inside readily defended walls, just in case enemy forces somehow successfully penetrated the defenses of the Citadel.

The well is still there, hidden beneath a trapdoor in the floorboards of Casement 18. It is rarely open to the public but I was given a private tour of the Citadel, and I was told the last time somebody had opened the trapdoor, the funk that emanated from the well was a foul, malodorous, and quite unholy reek.

No wonder.

Back in the winter of 1889, when the stink was first noticed, an investigation was ordered. The investigating troops discovered a man's decomposing arm tangled in a chain the depths of the well. That decomposing arm was wearing the rotted sleeve of a military tunic, with the deteriorating badge of a colour-sergeant stitched into the faded red fabric.

For years after, the weird apparition of that angry, one-armed colour-sergeant has been spotted standing stiffly at attention beside the well. If I use the powers of my sick and twisted storytelling imagination I can hear him standing there shouting, "Present, arm!"

34: Ghosts of the Halifax Explosion

ON THE NIGHT OF DECEMBER 5, 1917, the French vessel *Mont Blanc* pulled up outside of Halifax Harbour. Its captain, Aimé Le Médec, was in a foul mood. He'd arrived too late to meet the convoy that was to escort his vessel across the Atlantic Ocean. The anti-submarine nets keeping the German U-boats out of Halifax Harbour were pulled across the harbour for the evening. No one was allowed to come or go until morning.

He had a good reason for his foul disposition: his ship was a floating bomb, carrying three thousand tons of high explosives, including TNT, picric acid, gun cotton, and Benzol, a highly flammable fuel. Worse yet, *Mont Blanc* flew no flags warning of her cargo for fear of attracting the unwanted attention of a German U-boat's torpedoes.

Meanwhile, inside the netted Bedford Basin, the Belgian relief ship *Imo* waited to head out in the morning. Coal for her boilers had arrived too late for her to leave that day. Captain Haakon From was also behind schedule. His ship was heading to New York to collect emergency supplies for civilians in war-torn Belgium. A large sign was painted on her side: BELGIAN RELIEF. The captain prayed the sign would keep his ship in one piece.

Turns out it didn't.

The harbour opened at 7:30 A.M. and the *Mont Blanc* headed in, travelling at about four knots, well within the speed limit of five knots. Her warning flag still hadn't been raised. Meanwhile the *Imo* headed for the Narrows, increasing her speed to seven knots, keen as Captain From was to get going. This was right about the time *Imo* met the *Mont Blanc*.

Mont Blanc blew her whistle once, signalling she had the right of way and would maintain course. The *Imo* blew her whistle twice in reply, signalling her intent to stay *her* course. What followed was a piercing flurry of whistles between the two ships as they played a game of nautical chicken. At the very last minute, *Mont Blanc* turned hard to port and the *Imo* reversed hard astern.

At 8:45 A.M., the *Imo*'s prow struck the starboard side of the *Mont Blanc*. The prow narrowly missed the hold carrying the volatile TNT, but in an accidental ship-to-ship shoulder check, the *Imo* grazed and ground up against the hull of the *Mont Blanc*, buckling the *Mont Blanc*'s bow plates inwards by about three metres. It hit just hard enough to create a spark that ignited the barrels of Benzol, which in turn set off the highly unstable picric acid.

A tendril of smoke erupted out of the gash in the *Mont Blanc*'s hull. A fire started and grew rapidly. A cloud of oily black smoke enveloped the deck. *Mont Blanc*'s crew panicked and abandoned ship, climbing into a dory and rowing for the Dartmouth shore, yelling in French about the explosion they knew was imminent.

At 9:04:35 A.M., *Mont Blanc* erupted with a force stronger than any man-made explosion ever before. The steel hull burst sky-high, falling in a blizzard of red-hot, twisted projectiles on Dartmouth and Halifax. Some pieces were tiny, others breathtakingly huge. Part of the anchor hit the ground more than four kilometres away on the far side of Northwest Arm. A gun barrel landed in

Dartmouth more than five kilometres from the harbour. The force of the explosion flattened buildings and shattered glass windows. A white cloud billowed 20,000 feet above the city. The two square kilometres surrounding Pier 6 were flattened. More than 1,500 people were killed outright; hundreds more died in the days that followed. Nine thousand people, many of whom might have been safe if they hadn't come to watch the fire, were injured by the blast, falling buildings, and flying shards of glass.

The blast also triggered a tsunami eighteen metres high on the Halifax side. The water rushed over the shoreline, through the dockyard and beyond Campbell Road, which is now known as Barrington Street.

The resulting mini tsunami threw the *Imo* up out of the water and onto the Dartmouth shore. The ship stayed there until spring. The *Mont Blanc* was obliterated by the force of the blast, blown into thousands of wooden and steel shards, one of which turned up embedded in the walls of a Halifax church.

The *Imo* was blown ashore by the force of the explosion. Almost all of the crew were killed, but by the following July she was refurbished to serve as a whale-oil tanker. Her name was changed to the *Guvernören*, and she was sent south, never to return to Halifax.

Four years later the *Guvernören* grounded herself on a remote beach near Cape Carysfort, just off of the Falkland Islands. Her rusted iron bones still lay beached there today, watched over by the occasional tourist and a flock of Emperor Penguin, almost eleven thousand kilometres away from her place in history—Halifax, Nova Scotia.

Believe you me, there are thousands of memories of this fateful explosion that still haunt the city of Halifax, but let me tell you about a couple of the ghost stories that sprung up from out of the heart of the Halifax Explosion. (See stories 35 to 38.)

35: The Whispering Dead of the Chebucto Road School
44.6501° N, 63.5975° W

EARLY METEOROLOGISTS, INSPIRED BY TALES of torrential rainfall following battles waged during the Civil War and the Napoleonic Wars, came to believe that clouds could be shook up by battle enough to trigger a rainstorm. Whether you believe an artillery barrage can bring on rain, the weather that followed the Halifax Explosion was a good demonstration of that theoretical weather phenomenon.

The day after the Halifax Explosion the city was hit with a record-breaking snowfall. Mind you, meteorologists now know that the blizzard was forming long before the city-smashing blast. Remember, satellites and cable television weren't around back then. Over forty centimetres of snow fell on the morning of December 7. That was nothing compared to White Juan (February 2014), but when you dump that much snow on top of demolished city filled with blind, deafened, shell-shocked citizens you are in for a real mess.

People took shelter wherever they could. There were over twelve thousand buildings damaged or destroyed. Shelter was at a premium, not only for the living but also for the dead.

The Chebucto Road School, being a large and relatively undamaged building, was used first as a triage and first-aid centre. Shortly afterward, the school served as a morgue, as people in the first-aid centre succumbed to injury and lack of proper medical facilities. The authorities were doing the best they could, but the explosion had already killed more than two thousand people and left three times that many homeless.

They had to improvise.

No one had ever planned for a disaster such as this.

The basement of the schoolhouse gradually evolved from being used as a morgue into a makeshift funeral home. Coffins were carried in and out and a team of priests and ministers hastily administered whatever finally rites were thought most apt.

An event like this is bound to leave an impression on young minds.

For decades afterwards the students of the Chebucto Road School tried their very best to avoid spending too much time in the basement—even though the student washrooms were located down there.

"There are ghosts," more than one student claimed. "We can hear them whispering in the shadows and moving in the darkness."

In 1975, the school closed. The building became home to the Halifax Board of School Commissioners' Music Department. It now houses the Maritime Conservatory of Performing Arts. The conservatory has since renovated the assembly hall, which is now known as the Lilian Piercey Concert Hall. I haven't heard of any recently reported hauntings, but perhaps the ghosts have learned to appreciate good music.

36: The Haunted Window
of St. Paul's
44.6474° N, 63.5745° W

THE PROBLEM WITH SETTING UP a comprehensive ghost guide is you invariably find yourself treading upon a lot of familiar footsteps. Nearly everyone knows about this church, but not everyone knows the whole story behind its haunted window, which is often confused with the tale of the black window on the Robie Street Witch House.

The story behind the Haunted Window of St. Paul's Anglican Church is that the silhouette of a man can be clearly seen from the Argyle Street sidewalk, and that the silhouette belongs to a young unnamed church organist who was practicing on the great brass-piped church organ on the morning of the Halifax Explosion. Either the titanic force of the blast or a flying shard of stained glass decapitated the young organist, depending upon who tells the story. His head was blasted directly through what is now known as "the explosion window." The window has reportedly been replaced at least three times in the past century; each time, the face mysteriously reappears.

Of course, like every ghost story in the world, this tale has mutated with each retelling. The online magazine *Atlas Obscura* states that it was an anonymous sailor's decapitated head, hurled across the harbour and into the church by the massive force of the explosion, that smashed the haunted window. I'm not quite sure how the sailor's head would have possibly entered the church without breaking through a wall before it wound up smashing through the haunted window—but the internet never tells a lie, now does it?

In addition to the mysterious window silhouette, a piece of the *Imo* is imbedded above the church's memorial entrance doors. I've seen the shard and it is impressive; however, according to a St. Paul's Church tour guide with whom I spoke, the origin of the shard is a little closer at hand than the harbour itself.

"The story that the shard in the wall came from the *Imo* is nothing more than urban legend," the guide informed me. "The truth is the shard is actually a piece of metal windowsill blasted off a neighbouring building. The windowsill blasted through an Argyle Street window and drove itself into the opposite wall like a hard-flung javelin."

Truth or story, St. Paul's Anglican Church is still one of the earliest official structures to be raised in the city of Halifax and as such is well worth taking a look at.

It's a breathtakingly beautiful building and there are tour guides available throughout the summer who are happy to help you out with a story or two.

Besides, I don't know about you, but I have always preferred the song of a sweetly told story as opposed to the cold and hard bones of truth.

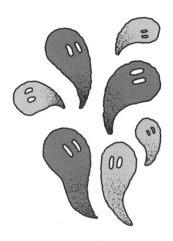

37: Ghosts of the Five Fishermen Restaurant

44.6479° N, 63.5754° W

WHILE YOU'RE ON YOUR DO-IT-YOURSELF haunted tour of the city of Halifax you're bound to get hungry. You might want to stop off at a local restaurant for a bite to eat. One of the most famous of all of the haunted restaurant locations in Halifax would definitely be the Five Fishermen Restaurant. The restaurant now stands in a building that originally was the home of Halifax's busiest undertaking business, the Snow & Company Undertaker. First founded in 1883 and still in business today as J.A. Snow Funeral Home, it is the oldest funeral home company in the city.

Snow & Company served as much as any funeral home could manage to, through two of Halifax's greatest tragedies. In 1912 the funeral home was responsible for the preparation and burying of many of the dead from the fateful wreck of the RMS *Titanic*.

Then, in 1917, Snow & Company were similarly responsible for the preparation and burial of many of the dead of the Halifax Explosion. During that sad time, Snow & Company conducted approximately three dozen funeral services a day!

Business was definitely booming, so it is no wonder the building is considered haunted by spirits from both tragedies.

The employees of the Five Fisherman Restaurant will happily support that history with actual ghost stories of their own. I had the chance to talk with some of the employees one October evening back in 2014 while I was there to take part in a CTV television spot.

The ghost of a beautiful young woman has been seen standing upon the staircase, one of the servers told me. "Her eyes looked so very beautiful and yet so very sad, like pools of rainwater," the server told me the night I first visited the restaurant. "I just couldn't make myself look away."

Another server told me about a young dishwasher's first night on the job. Late and alone, the dishwasher scrubbed pots and pans in the restaurant's dish pit. The cupboard doors rattled and slammed. Startled, the young dishwasher looked up to see a ghostly apparition drifting through the kitchen.

"It was like watching an empty plastic garbage bag blowing down an abandoned street," he said. "That's exactly what he told me. It was just a big shape moving around the kitchen. Each of the cupboards opened and closed, like it was looking for something. That dishwasher bolted out of the building and never returned. He phoned in the next day and asked to have his last paycheque mailed out to him."

"I'm not sure what he thought he saw," Wallace Fraser, the manager of the Five Fishermen reported. "He swore to me over the telephone that he saw something but he wouldn't tell me just exactly what he saw.

"That's just how it goes at this restaurant," Fraser went on to say. "We always say you can stay late if you've got work to do, but you never ought to stay here alone."

A few years before the interview, I spoke with another employee who told me of seeing the ghost of a white-haired ship's captain dressed in a long black greatcoat. He saw the captain standing on the second-floor landing.

"I thought he was waiting to be served. Then I noticed somebody had knocked over an ashtray," he told me, which indicates just how long ago it really was. "When I stood back up from picking up the ashtray, I could see nothing but the reflection of this tall old man with his long, flowing, silvery hair and wearing a long black coat—then he was gone."

Dishes have flown through the air, cutlery has been found stuck in the walls of the kitchen, and one of the spirits plays tricks with the lights. Scarier still is the tale that another server told me about how she had once seen the figure of a young child standing completely INSIDE of the great wall mirror that still hangs today in the main dining room.

"When we close up at night, we try to have at least two servers on because of all the bizarre things that seem to happen," Five Fishermen server Mallory LeBlanc said to the CTV interviewer, Suzette Belliveau.

"At the end of the night, when people are starting to go home and it gets more quiet, you kind of stop trying to hear things because you're afraid of what you're going to hear," added server Jill Baker.

I guess I cannot really blame either of them. Still, the Five Fishermen offers some of the best seafood eating you can find here in Halifax.

38: The Halifax Explosion Memorial Bell Tower

44.6657°N 63.6012°W

YOU SHOULD ALSO BE SURE to take a good look at the Halifax Explosion Memorial Bell Tower, located in Fort Needham Park in North End Halifax, overlooking the region of the city, then known as Richmond, that was most devastated by the explosion. The memorial exists to not only to honour and to commemorate those thousands of Haligonians who lost their lives in the explosion, but also help to remember the many survivors who worked together to rebuild Halifax, Dartmouth, and surrounding areas.

The sixty-foot-tall memorial is mounted on a granite platform and is primarily built out of what the designers referred to as "monolithic hydrostone," a form of concrete mixed with crushed granite and originally produced at a plant in Eastern Passage. The memorial was constructed in the shape of a blasted building and is adorned with sturdy brass flashing and a carillon of ten huge church bells. The ten brass bells had originally been donated back in 1921 to the United Memorial Church by Barbara Orr, in memory of her entire family who had been tragically lost in the Halifax Explosion. The inscription engraved upon each of the bells reads: "In memoriam—Samuel Orr and his wife Annie S. Orr, and their children Ian, Mary, Archie, Isabel, and James, who departed this life December 6, 1917—presented by their daughter Barbara, 1920."

The United Memorial Church, which stood at 5735 Kaye Street in Halifax for over ninety years before it closed in 2016, had been originally built to replace the two churches lost in the Halifax Explosion: the Kaye Street Methodist Church and Grove Presbyterian Church. The two churches had been completely obliterated, along with over two hundred parishioners.

Many of the surviving church members had been scarred or blinded by the blast. The remainder of the two congregations decided to work together to raise the funds necessary to construct a new church. For a time, the two congregations met once a week, celebrating services at a temporary building at the intersection of Young and Gottingen Streets that came to be known locally as the "tarpaper church."

Construction on the new church began in 1920 and on September 18, 1921, a dedication ceremony was held and the new church was officially opened. At that time the upstairs portion of the United Memorial Church remained unfinished, and the very first service had to be held in the basement, in what eventually came to be known as the Sunday School Room. As well as the donated church bells, the church also possessed a set of magnificent stained-glass windows, a huge brass pipe organ, and a beautiful baptismal font—all donated and individually dedicated in the memory of the victims killed in the terrible explosion.

However, in the mid-1960s growing structural damage was noticed in the church belfry and the memorial bells had to be removed. They were unceremoniously placed upon the front lawn of the church, crudely protected by heavy industrial tarpaulins, until their final fate could be decided. Eventually the bells were donated and installed in the Halifax Explosion Memorial Bell Tower in Needham Park, and they were first rung at that new location in June of 1985. Several years later, four more bells were added.

The Bell Tower will always have a special place in my heart because my wife and I walked up to enjoy the peace and quiet on a crisp autumn morning right before our wedding ceremony at the Family Courthouse on Devonshire Avenue. The bells rang while we were up there and I always felt that it was a beautiful omen for our future as a couple.

So far, so good.

The Halifax Explosion Memorial Bell Tower similarly has a very special place in the heart of Halifax. There is an annual remembrance ceremony is held at the Memorial Bell Tower on every December 6 morning, followed by a short ceremonial silence that takes place just before 9:05 A.M., the exact time of the Halifax Explosion.

A Terrible Misprint

Although there have been no ghosts sighted in the park, there was a terrible misprint that remained there for many years. The plaque originally placed at the foot of the memorial read as follows:

On the morning of December 6, 1917, the French munitions ship Mont Blanc, inbound for a brief stop on her way from New York to the war in Europe with a cargo of benzol, gun cotton, picric acid and TNT, collided with the outbound Belgian relief ship Imo. Reversing her engines, Mont Blanc went astern to pull out the deep gash in Imo's side: steel rasped against ragged steel, sparks flew, Mont Blanc caught fire and blew up at 9:04:35 a.m.

The toll of identifiable dead, ashore and in ships, was 1,963; more than 9,000 others suffered injuries, often to carry their marks and scars for life. Many of the northern parts of Halifax and Dartmouth were devastated. Phoneix-like, they rose again, stronger and finer, from the ashes.

Look east, down the hill, towards Dartmouth on the opposite shore, in line with the opening between two sections of the explosion Memorial. You are looking at the place in the harbour Narrows where the most violent man-made explosion before the atomic bomb occurred there in 1917.

That is the original inscription, word for word. The major typo occurred in the very first paragraph where it reads: "Reversing her engines, Mont Blanc went astern to pull out the deep gash in Imo's side." As you might remember from your history lessons (or just from earlier in this book), it was the *Imo* that reversed her engines to pull astern, causing the sparks that set off the explosion within the *Mont Blanc*'s deadly cargo. Besides that critical factual error, the plaque-maker misspelled "phoenix" as "phoneix."

I know, I am being picky, but believe it or not, that plaque stood there in front of the monument for seventeen years. People noticed it and some even complained, but the wheels of bureaucracy are often sadly slow in turning.

For those of you who have read through this whole entire section, I apologize deeply for not being able to give you any weird or ghostly anecdotes about this location. Still, if you stand on this hill as the bells ring out over the skyline and across the water I guarantee that the sleeping memories of this massive explosion will stir within you.

39: The Henry House Heebie-Jeebie

44.6404° N, 63.5708° W

A NOTHER HALIFAX DINING ESTABLISHMENT THAT has reputation for being haunted is The Henry House.

This stately 1834 two-and-a-half-storey structure is built out of locally quarried ironstone and granite shipped all the way from Scotland. The original owner, John Metzler, was a well known landowner and stonemason who had been commissioned to work on the mighty stone fortifications of Fort George, on Citadel Hill.

Twenty years later, the building was purchased by William Alexander Henry, one of the Fathers of Confederation and a co-author of the British North America Act, a provincial attorney general, a member of the Nova Scotia House of Assembly, a mayor of Halifax, and the first Nova Scotian to serve as a justice of the Supreme Court of Canada.

When Henry sold the building in 1864, it was used as a home for retired sailors, operated by the Halifax branch of the Navy

League of Canada. In 1968 it was sold to Dick Raymond and Jacques Ducau, who did extensive renovations and opened The Henry House restaurant on the upper floor. The downstairs was known as The Little Stone Jug. It was at that time that the building was declared a National Historic Site and it has been the home of fine Halifax dining ever since.

And, according to Bill and Donna Alsop, the current owners of The Henry House, it is also the home to several different ghosts.

For starters, there are the beer taps. Apparently, they are haunted. On several occasions, even back before the current owners purchased the building, the beer taps would open suddenly, pouring perfectly good beer down the drain. There was no apparent reason for this odd manifestation. There were no electronic components to malfunction. The taps, in order to open, had to be physically turned by hand.

All that beer down the drain—oh, the humanity!

In addition, the ghost of a lovely Irish kitchen maid has been seen both by the owners and several late-night pedestrians. Sometimes she is seen standing outside of the building, either in the driveway or on the Barrington Street sidewalk, while other times the mystery woman has been spotted on the main stairway inside of the building itself. The one distinctive feature mentioned by every single one of the witnesses is her long, cascading, midnight-black hair.

Lastly, there is the spirit of a young girl who has been occasionally seen, but more often heard. You can see her photograph hanging in the main entrance of the restaurant. In it she is riding with her family in a horse-drawn carriage.

Apparently the girl was the daughter of a gentleman who worked in the Navy League. Sadly, the young girl died from a bad case of whooping cough.

Employees have reported sudden extreme drops in temperature—and that is when they know that the spirit of the young girl is amongst them. Occasionally they hear her calling out for her mother or father. Other times they hear her coughing.

As of yet, there has never been any sensation of menace reported around this particular apparition. Witnesses simply feel her presence and an unmistakable aura of loneliness. She is a little girl who dearly misses her parents.

So, the next time that you feel the need for a little home-grown Nova Scotia pub food mixed with a taste of the paranormal, be certain to pay a visit to the Henry House. I would recommend the locally brewed dark ale known as Peculiar, as well as the homemade bread pudding.

40: The Ghost of the Halifax Armoury

44.6516° N, 63.5870° W

THE HALIFAX ARMOURY WAS DESIGNED in 1895 by Chief Dominion Architect Thomas Fuller, the very same fellow who designed the original Parliament Building in Ottawa that was lost to fire in 1916. If you look at the Armoury today, you will see something that looks exactly like one more big old medieval castle–type structure. But way back when it was first built in the 1890s, it was actually considered to be one of the more sophisticated structures in the whole entire country. In fact, the Armoury was one of the first buildings here in Halifax to be wired for electricity.

I have a great fondness for the building on account of the fact that one of my earliest years in Halifax was spent working there. Back then I was attending the University of King's College and I served a whole year with the Princess Louise Fusiliers. Now, I can't tell you much more about that time in my life except that I spent an awful lot of time doing push-ups on a cold concrete floor. I am pretty certain the echoes of some of my push-up shouts are still reverberating within the walls of the Halifax Armoury.

Of course, you could probably say the same thing about the echoes of an awful lot of Canadian soldiers. You have to remember that back in the days of the world wars there were an awful lot of soldiers who passed through those big wooden front doors. Remember, Halifax was basically the front door to Europe back then.

The Halifax Armoury served as a transit point for many of the Canadian troops who sailed to Europe throughout the Boer War and both world wars, even though the building was seriously damaged back in 1917 during the Halifax Explosion when the west wall was displaced, moving a whole two feet by the force of the blast. In spite of the structural damage, the Armoury provided shelter for many of the folks who had lost their homes, including my great-grandmother, who took shelter there during the cold winter blizzard that followed the Halifax Explosion.

In January 2017—one hundred years since that fateful blast— the necessary renovations needed to restore the west wall back to its original position finally began, and by all reports should be completed by 2019 as the crow flies.

Don't ever tell me the Government of Nova Scotia doesn't know how to take its good old time at getting things done. Alexander Keith—a man who believed in taking the time to get his beer right—doesn't have a thing on our politicians. Even snails move faster than that.

The Ghost of the Halifax Armoury

Here I go again, talking all about history when all you really opened this book up for was a ghost story. Well let me tell you: the Armoury does have a great ghost story behind it. It is said to be haunted by a single lonely ghost who is reported to be dressed in the uniform of a First World War–era Canadian soldier. This one lonely soldier has never left his post; he still patrols the far end of the building. Some folks have seen his spirit marching in the shadows of the far wall, while others have seen the flicker of his lantern glowing from within the darker corners of the building.

Sometimes you can see him standing in the shadows, and sometimes witnesses have reported hearing the echoes of his marching feet, still keeping time after all of those long and lonely years of military vigil.

Not much is known about the soldier's life, excepting that it has been recorded he served faithfully and had returned home from the war only to find his wife had left him for another man. He was said to have committed suicide shortly thereafter. His body was interred, yet his spirit continues to return to his post.

41: The Bayers Lake Mystery Walls

44° 38' 34.8" N, 63° 39' 32.4" W

SOMETIMES THE STRANGEST OF MYSTERIES can be hidden right in plain sight, and you never know they're there.

The Bayers Lake Mystery Walls have been hidden from public knowledge for over two hundred years and it only came to our city's attention back in October 1990, when a Bedford carpet cleaner and amateur historian by the name of Jack McNab contacted the Halifax Museum and the *Chronicle Herald* as well as any local politician who had the time to listen to him, asking them to intercede and to prevent the hidden historical site from being bulldozed under by construction crews of the newly developed and constantly growing Bayers Lake Business Park.

Directly across the street from the building that houses the FX101.9 and 89.9 radio stations, the city has carved out just enough space for a handful of cars to park beside the entrance to the hiking trail that leads you down through the lonely Nova Scotia woods to the Bayers Lake Mystery Walls.

Now let me give you a warning right off the bat: this isn't a location for the unprepared. Until the city decides to properly develop the site, this is a trip for only the most seasoned of hikers. In fact, the very first time I visited the location I got lost for a while. Well, maybe I wasn't exactly lost, but I was fearfully confused for a good hour or so, and I am pretty sure there were some birds and rabbits laughing at my intense discomfort.

The good news is that I did have a pretty solid idea on just which way the radio station was situated from where I was standing and scratching my head, but it could have easily gone a whole lot differently. All kidding aside, you really need to dress for the hike, and do not expect to find any clear paths and easy travelling. A pair of good (waterproof) hiking boots is an absolute necessity and you might also want to bring a high-quality working compass or else a portable GPS device with you.

The unmortared ironstone slate wall crawls along the hillside like a gigantic stone and moss-ridden caterpillar for over two-hundred metres in length and about three feet in height. The very first time I saw this wall, I thought to myself this edifice must surely have been the result of a group of restless and imaginative kids—but the sheer amount of physical labour that went into the construction of this wall would have required an entire army of hyperactive masonry-inclined teenagers and several intense years of hard labour.

Some folks believe the stone wall was built by a local farmer, but the surrounding terrain would grow nothing more than possibly an acre or two of scruffy wild blueberries. It is just too hilly and too rocky, and the tall pine trees speak of an acidic soil that would be of little use to any sort of grain or vegetable crop.

Mind you, there is always the chance this wall was something built by an eighteenth- or nineteenth-century farmer. After all, the farms back then were a lot smaller. Folks couldn't easily tend large acreages, but if I had to place a solid wager on the actual origins of these strange stone structures, I would have to say that an over-protective farmer would be my very last guess.

Along with the stone wall there is a mysterious five-sided structure that has puzzled many curious hikers. To my eye, the stone building looks an awful lot like a crude replica of a five-sided bastion, most commonly used in a typical fifteenth-century European star fortress. The advantage of the five sides meant that the structure, when facing an oncoming siege, had absolutely no dead space whatsoever. Anyone in the open ground between two of those five-sided bastions was easy prey.

So, it is my opinion that the structure was built partly as a makeshift—and possibly a make-work—project for the local military. The wall does, in effect, cover the whole back door of the old Halifax settlements. It also would have served as a dandy training ground, where British troops could either practise up on their siege techniques, or else test out their defensive maneuvers and run drills.

Neither of these theories, however, can readily explain the long stone staircase to nowhere that climbs over twenty metres straight up the hillside, apparently leading nowhere in particular.

Still, I am just guessing at the origin of this mysterious structure.

That is the really cool thing about this sight. The mysterious stonework truly is an honest-to-who-done-it mystery. We may never know just exactly when and why these walls were built, nor does it hint at just who actually built them. In fact, this story may never truly find an ending.

In December of 1998, a provincial lichenologist—someone who makes a career of studying moss and lichen—took a long hard look at the lichen growths clinging to the dry stonework walls, and concluded that the growth had not been disturbed since around the year 1798. So, two hundred years' worth of mystery and we still do not have a clear-cut answer. It is definitely worth seeing, even though it is hard to access.

I will leave you with this one note: if you do travel there, do *not* leave any trash behind. Do not climb the walls, because the rocks do not have mortar, and might easily slip. Do not give in to the temptation to move or steal any of the rocks. This is a very special location and you should do your utmost to keep it looking just exactly as what when you first see it. Feel free to take pictures and gather memories or fodder for stories, but nothing else.

42: The Spring Garden Road
Memorial Public Library
44.6442° N, 63.5747° W

ALTHOUGH THE FACILITIES CLOSED AS of August 30, 2014, the Spring Garden Road Memorial Public Library will always hold a horde of fond memories for me. Heck, I did some of the research for my very first ghost-story collection in the reference department of this wonderful old library. I miss that closed-in, musky, tunnel feeling the narrow winding corridors always gave me. I miss the random heaps of comic books and the shelves crammed with magazines and books.

Don't get me wrong: I love the new Halifax Central Library situated across the street from the old library. I love the well-lit roominess of the new library and the coffee shops on both the main floor and the top floor. The coffee is good and dark and strong, and they make a totally wonderful breakfast muffin that I am sadly addicted to.

But I want to talk about the old library, on the corner of Spring Garden Road and Grafton Street. Although the building is tucked in from the street side you really can't miss it. Just look for the building that Winston Churchill is striding in front of.

Some of you folks may have heard of the ghost that prowls this old building. Probably some of you have heard how some of the older library employees have reported hearing creaks and groans and footsteps, and some have even heard the sounds of a slow, raspy, and almost asthmatic phantom breathing in the shadows long after the library closed for the night.

Some of you folks may even know the story of what public institution the library property used to be home to.

The Halifax Poor House

Back in 1758, the Halifax Poor House stood where the Spring Garden Memorial Public Library now stands. The Poor House served as sort of a halfway step to the Halifax Jail, in that it housed Halifax's "unacceptable" caste. If you were a drunkard, fortune-teller, panhandler, runaway, orphan, or—God help you—a Sabbath-breaker, you might find yourself sentenced to reside for a spell within the dingy walls of the Halifax Poor House.

And this was definitely not a pleasant stay.

A whipping post and a set of heavy wooden stocks stood in plain sight on the front lawn of the Halifax Poor House. Public floggings were regular events and there were often people leaning uncomfortably day in and day out in the confines of the heavy wooden punishment stocks. While making a surprise inspection, noted Nova Scotian Joseph Howe was startled to discover a male resident of the Halifax Poor House chained to the iron fence with a fierce-looking spiked leather collar worn uncomfortably around his neck.

Those who were forced to live within the walls of the Poor House suffered very short and hard lives, but their punishment did not end with their eventual demise. The dead were unceremoniously buried in shallow graves beneath the front lawn.

Casual pedestrians had to be wary of crossing the lawn for fear of tripping over an exposed arm or leg.

By all reports it was a charnel house and a public atrocity. It wasn't a nice place to visit and you *definitely* would not want to stay there.

The Ghost of the Spring Garden Road Memorial Library

Eventually the authorities decided the Poor House was unsightly and would be better off located somewhere less central. The Poor House was torn down and the ad hoc graveyard was covered in a deep layer of black earth. People just did their very best to forget about the whole thing. Trees and shrubs were planted, park benches installed, and the place was even given the euphemistic name of Grafton Park.

Then, in 1951, a new set of authorities decided a public library would be the perfect use of for the property. The Spring Garden Road Memorial Library was raised over the ruins of the Halifax Poor House and drop-in graveyard.

The librarians began to notice the creaks, groans, wheezes, and footsteps; they blamed it on a ghost. Most of you folks have probably heard the story right up until this point—but have you heard who the Spring Garden Road Memorial Library ghost *really* was?

Was the ghost an ex-employee?

Or perhaps the ghost was merely a client of the library?

Perhaps the ghost was an addicted reader, tormented by the guilt of an overdue library book, sadly forgotten beneath their death bed?

All of these are good possibilities. However, there is another theory that presents itself.

The little-known-yet-oddly-famous Quebec author, Philippe Aubert de Gaspé Junior, author of the very first French-Canadian novel, fled from Quebec to Halifax following a terrible literary scandal and a big stink.

Let me tell you how the story goes.

Philippe Aubert de Gaspé worked as a journalist for the Quebec newspapers *Quebec Mercury* and *Le Canadien*. In November 1835, Gaspé was charged with journalistic plagiarism and sentenced to a month in prison. Following his release in February 1836, Gaspé set off a stink bomb filled with asafoetida, a strong-smelling herb, in the halls of the National Assembly of Quebec.

That would be your big stink.

Fleeing the scene of his rather childish prank and the possibility of even more jail time, Philippe Aubert de Gaspé fled Quebec and found sanctuary in the Halifax home of his father, Philippe Aubert de Gaspé Senior, a local public official. It was here Gaspé wrote his first and only novel, *L'influence d'un livre* or in English, *The Influence of a Book*.

Unfortunately, Gaspé's father made a few bad financial choices and was thrown into jail over a matter of unpaid debts; Philippe's money situation became troublesome. Philippe Junior was forced to take up a job in the Halifax Poor House. He was employed as a teacher to the orphans who were also kept in the poorhouse. At the same time he subsidized his income by writing occasional articles for the local newspaper.

It wasn't a good living. His health suffered and inevitably failed. At the age of twenty-seven, Philippe Aubert de Gaspé was buried on the poorhouse property—so in a very real way, you could say Philippe Aubert de Gaspé's personal solid-brick tombstone was the Spring Garden Road Memorial Public Library.

According to the one librarian I spoke to, "if the old library is indeed haunted, it would most likely be haunted by the ghost of Philippe Aubert de Gaspé."

I don't know about you, but I would make my book on that theory.

43: The George Street Celtic Cross
44°38'55"N 63°34'20"W

THE TWELVE-FOOT-HIGH GRANITE CELTIC CROSS was presented to the city of Halifax by the Charitable Irish Society on March 17, 2000. According to the inscription, the George Street Celtic Cross is "dedicated to the original Irish settlers of 1749 and to the contributions of the Irish community to Halifax, to Nova Scotia and to Canada."

In 2016, the Charitable Irish Society added to the Celtic Cross memorial by commissioning a brand new commemorative plaque to mark the one hundredth anniversary of the 1916 Easter Uprising of Ireland. The plaque was placed at the base of the great stone cross and features an Easter lily, the symbol of both insurrection and remembrance.

These are noble sentiments indeed but it just so happens the George Street Celtic Cross is also located very close to the place where Halifax's very first public gallows was erected, and where the very first public hanging in Nova Scotia—in fact, in Canada itself—took place.

The Hanging of Peter Carteel

Back in the early days of Halifax, while the first settlers were still waiting upon the ships to settle ashore, a French-born sailor by the name of Peter Carteel (sometimes written as Peter Cartcel or Peter Carsal) pulled a four-inch fishing knife on boatswain's mate Abraham Goodsides in the midst of an argument on the deck of the transport vessel *Beaufort*.

Well, to be fair the argument was a little unbalanced, given that Peter Carteel spoke very little English and Goodsides's entire rebuttal consisted of him slapping Carteel across the cheek, which encouraged Carteel to pull out said fishing knife and jam the blade into Abraham Goodsides's chest. Carteel also cut two other men during a struggle to escape.

The trial was a hasty affair that took place in a warehouse, one of the only buildings that had actually been completely built back then. Governor Edward Cornwallis, acting hastily, named himself and six councillors to try the case. Mind you, neither the councillors nor Cornwallis had any sort of legal training, and then there was that whole language issue, with Peter Carteel speaking very little English and the councillors (and Cornwallis as well) speaking absolutely no French at all.

Of course, maybe they didn't think they needed all that much in the way of legal training seeing that no one bothered to provide a lawyer to represent Peter Carteel. I mean, why waste time with legal representation when you have a big old city to construct?

A jury of twelve citizens—several of them being shipmates of Abraham Goodsides—were commissioned to decide Peter Carteel's fate. Four witnesses came forward—two of them shipmates of Goodsides—and related what they had seen.

It probably did not help that the fourth witness was a Halifax police constable by the name of Roger Snowden, who testified that

Carteel and Goodsides had been seen to be engaged in a fierce argument earlier that day before the stabbing even took place.

"There was bad blood," Snowden stated. "It was plain to see that there was very little love lost between the two men."

Peter Carteel asked witness James Gordon, with the help of his court-appointed translator, if it were at all possible that Abraham Goodsides might have accidentally tripped, or inadvertently fallen, or run up against the knife blade, thus possibly killing himself.

"No sir," Gordon replied. "I saw that you did it."

James Gordon went on to explain how Peter Carteel had taken two deliberate steps backwards before delivering a powerful hooking backhand slash with his blade.

Thirty minutes later, Peter Carteel was convicted of murder. Carteel was sentenced to be hanged two days later on September 2.

When those two days had passed they threw a rope over a large hardwood tree, situated just outside of the warehouse that had served as both courtroom and crime scene—right about where that Celtic Cross now stands and they hung Peter Carteel.

The tree stood and served as Halifax's very own hanging tree until 1763, when it was cut down and a proper gallows was erected. For years afterwards, a shadowy figure some believe to be the ghost of Peter Carteel has been seen in the lower George Street area, perhaps searching for a little justice or possibly just looking for his lost fishing knife. There are others who swear they have seen the shadow of a hanging figure looming across that darkened street corner.

44: Double Alex at the Maritime Museum of the Atlantic

44.6475° N, 63.5708° W

T HIS IS A STORY THAT the Maritime Museum guides love to tell museum visitors every October. The funny thing is the story does not actually start in the museum; it only ends there.

The story begins back in 1758 when a lighthouse was commissioned for Sambro Island, situated at the very mouth of Halifax Harbour. The sixty-foot-tall stone tower contained a dim and flickering white light and a fellow by the name of Joseph Rous was appointed the building's very first lightkeeper. The lighthouse was a fine and beautiful structure and the light itself was truly state-of-the-art, fuelled as it was by only the finest and most pungent of whale oils.

The problem with whale oil was it left an oily residue on the glass of the light. In addition to the smudged-up residue, the moisture in the whale oil made frost upon the lighthouse glass a constant hazard. In 1772, the whale-oil-burning light was replaced with a far more dependable kerosene lantern, which smelled a little better as well.

Then, in 1833, a unit of light artillerymen were temporarily stationed on the island to help man the lighthouse and operate the signal cannons. The trouble got started when the commander of the unit decided to entrust his quartermaster sergeant with the unit's payroll and supply money.

That was a big old mistake.

It turned out that the quartermaster sergeant, whose name was actually Alex Alexander, or Double Alex as his friends always called him, was a man of very weak moral fibre. Now I am not saying old Double Alex was all that much of a bad guy, you understand. He was more along the lines of a man who is supposed to be on a diet deciding it would be a really good idea to sit himself directly down beside the party platter of Swedish meatballs, occasionally reaching for not-so-discreet handfuls. (And oh, yes: when I talk about problems of diet, etiquette, and Swedish meatballs I am *definitely* speaking from personal experience. Just ask my wife.)

Well, old Double Alex decided it'd be a really good idea to sit down at a tavern in Halifax before setting out on his supply run. And wouldn't you know it, but that day was hot and dry and wouldn't a tall cold mug of good draught beer go down smoothly on such a hot dry day, and by golly, you just can't have a mug or two of good cold beer without a helping of tavern wings—which back then were more likely to be pigeon or grouse wings—and by golly, you can't have an order of pigeon or grouse wings without an order of boiled potatoes to go along with the wings and beer, now can you?

And you ought to note that I am saying boiled potatoes, on account of French fries having not been invented just yet.

And before you knew it, old Double Alex woke up with his pockets emptied out, pasted face down in a plate full of cold boiled potatoes, and quicker than you could say throw-him-in-the-brig-Duffy, his commanding officer decided to have Double Alex locked up in the lighthouse, waiting for his first very own personal court martial.

"It's your just dessert, Alex," the commanding officer told him.

"I'm too full for dessert," Alex replied. "How about if we just skip the whole thing and call it a day?"

Only the commanding officer wasn't in the mood for skipping, so that night Double Alex decided to do his own kind of rope-work. He found himself a good length of a rope and decided what he was going to.

"I've come to the end of my rope," Double Alex said to himself. "So I might as well tie myself a gallows knot and hang with it."

The next morning, his commanding officer found Double Alex dangling from the rope and the rafters, about ten feet off of the lighthouse floorboards.

Well, for many decades afterwards, old Double Alex's ghost kept hanging around the Sambro Lighthouse. Kegs were overturned and footsteps were heard where feet weren't stepping, and doors slammed unexpectedly.

So you might be wondering just how come I have not bothered to put the Sambro Island Lighthouse on our Nova Scotia most-haunted ghost tour map?

I have two words for you: government funding.

It seems that back in 1906, the Nova Scotia government decided it was time to indulge in a little infrastructural upgrade. The Sambro Island Lighthouse was completely overhauled and the old kerosene lamp was replaced with a powerful new light that can be seen as far as twenty-three miles away. The old stonework was completely covered by wooden outer-coating, and the height of the lighthouse was increased by seven metres.

The original Sambro Lighthouse lens was given over to the care of the Maritime Museum of the Atlantic. In 1982, when the museum moved to its current location on the Halifax waterfront, the lighthouse lens moved with it and continues to be displayed prominently in the museum's lobby. It is one of the first things you see as you enter, standing there looking for all the world like some gigantic cybernetic robot owl's giant glass eye.

Ever since the move, museum employees report hearing strange creaks and groans throughout the lobby, and many have reported seeing the spirit of a man dressed in authentic nineteenth-century military garb. Might the ghost of Double Alex have accompanied the light? Many employees refuse to work late because of this odd phenomenon. Can you blame them?

Other Museum Ghosts

There is a life-sized marble statue of Captain James Augustus Farquhar standing in the front entrance of the Maritime Museum of the Atlantic, and for many years museum employees swore they could smell the funky odour of the captain's particular—and very peculiar—blend of pipe tobacco, which smelled a little bit like old tennis sneakers and wet dog.

In addition to the pipe-smoking statue, museum employees report seeing the ghosts of two young children whose last name was Moxon. The children had died in a cholera outbreak and were buried beneath two rustic wooden crosses. It took their parents several years of very hard work before they could afford to purchase an actual marble headstone to commemorate the memory of their dear departed children.

Unfortunately, the parents were killed during the Halifax Explosion before they ever got the chance to see the tombstone raised. The wooden crosses were blown away in the force of the blast, and the location of the Moxon grave forgotten. The marble tombstone is instead displayed in the museum, and employees swear the ghosts of the Moxon children often run and giggle in the darkness, usually very close to the tombstone.

45: The Old Halifax Courthouse

44°38'22.01"N, 63°34'14.81"W

I WROTE A FAIR BIT ABOUT the Halifax Courthouse in my earlier collection, *Halifax Haunts: Exploring the City's Spookiest Spaces.* A few months after that release, I was contacted by a gentleman who worked at the courthouse and was invited to actually tour the courthouse and to hear some of the eerie occurrences that certain employees reported. So let me tell you what I have learned, but first let me give those folks who haven't read *Halifax Haunts* a quick update on the background of this historic and haunted Halifax landmark.

The main section of the Halifax Courthouse was constructed out of sandstone from out of the belly of a Wallace, Nova Scotia, stone quarry, in 1863. The building was designed in the Italian Renaissance style by noted Toronto architectural firm William Thomas and Sons. The courthouse was one of the last major buildings Thomas ever personally designed, and it is somewhat interesting to note that he designed this structure at the very same time his firm was sketching the plans for the Don Jail in Toronto.

Stone was chosen for this structure following a series of fires that raged through Halifax. A rear wing was added to the courthouse in 1882 and a west and east wing were added to the structure in 1908 and 1931, respectively.

The Old Halifax Courthouse has been in service ever since, although the building of the new waterfront courthouse facilities resulted in the Old Courthouse being used only as a legal library from 1971 to 1985. However, in 1985 the growing demand for courthouse facilities necessitated the restoration of the Old Courthouse to working status. Trials have been held there ever since.

And through all of these years something has walked these stone walls.

What Haunts These Walls?

For many years, employees of the courthouse have reported odd happenings. A ghostly figure has been spotted in the attic. Objects are moved and lights play tricks upon the unwary, particularly late at night.

I have been up there in the attic and it is truly an eerie place. It is hot and dusty with a set of simple wooden stairs and rows of simple metal shelving that store filing boxes crammed with many decades worth of courthouse files. You walk carefully, for fear of crumbled brick and concrete and metal electric cables. There are a few pieces of discarded furniture and a few random mouse droppings. There is a small room where a caretaker once stayed; however, the room has long been unused. Apparently, the caretaker quit his job unexpectedly after seeing something eerie up there in the attic.

The cells in the lower half of the courthouse are still used and can easily hold approximately fifty residents. These cells have been strangely quiet, I was told. It is only in the upstairs attic where the sightings have occurred.

So, what lonely spirit haunts the attic? Some believe that it is the ghost of Daniel P. Sampson, the very last man to be hanged at the Old Halifax Courthouse.

Let me tell you about it.

The story begins on a summer evening in July 1933, after the bloodied bodies of two young brothers, Edward and Bramwell Heffernan, were discovered alongside the railroad tracks that ran close to their home, in the area now home to the Armdale Rotary.

After an extensive police investigation, charges were laid upon one Daniel P. Sampson: a forty-nine-year-old veteran of the First World War who was reported to suffer from a "diminished mental capacity" and possibly post-traumatic stress. He also could not read or write, which makes me wonder how a signed confession was obtained from this man.

In any case, on the evening of March 7, 1935, Daniel P. Sampson took his last walk towards the gallows that were situated outside the back of the courthouse, away from the public eye. The gallows were taken down shortly after that hanging, and there are quite a few people who claim some of the pieces of the gallows were stored in the courthouse attic.

And that is where the legend takes shape. People believe the spirit of Daniel P. Sampson still walks the courthouse area, particularly the attic. I did not see any trace of the old gallows. When I asked, I was told these tales were nothing more than a persistent rumour; there were no pieces of the gallows left over. Employees of the courthouse have asked this question many times and several of the employees have actually searched the attic for traces of the gallows, but there was nothing to be found.

I am still not convinced the pieces are not up there in spite of this assurance. After all, the gallows was a simple structure, built of basic lumber. The pieces that may have possibly been stored would have looked like nothing more than pieces of lumber to the casual onlooker's eye. The rope was usually shredded after a hanging, or cut into pieces and burned. Officials did not want to supply any sort of ghoulish memorabilia to casual souvenir seekers.

This lumber in turn might have simply been used as floorboards or utility shelves or any number of utilitarian uses.

I cannot prove it, and perhaps I am nothing more than a simple storyteller in search of a tale. Apparently the jury is still out on that particular verdict.

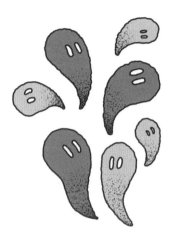

46: Dead on Delivery
44.6472° N, 63.5727° W

THERE IS A STORY PEOPLE have been telling around
Halifax for an awful lot of years now. It is a story of wealth
and power and the all-important practice of always keeping up
appearances.

Let me tell you a little bit about the Halifax Club.

In 1862 the club's original founders purchased the Hollis Street
building for the princely sum of eight thousand dollars. Ever since,
the upper-crust citizens of Halifax have been hanging their top
hats and opera capes at the Halifax Club. Back then the club was
a place reserved for the elite and privileged. The breath of scandal
never passed those heavy oak doors—or at the very least, was
never admitted to.

There was, of course, the 1870 story of James Forman, the
house steward who was caught embezzling funds and making off
with the silverware. When he was caught, the active committee

demanded the return of the missing funds. No charges would be pressed so long as Forman promised to quietly retire.

But James Forman wasn't big on doing things quietly, I guess.

It seems that during an evening gathering at the Halifax Club, Forman broke in and treated everyone to an impromptu sermon, in which he cursed out everyone in the building who had ears to listen. I believe he also used sign language for those folks with hearing difficulties.

Following the foul-mouthed rant, Forman punctuated his shout-out by stabbing himself repeatedly with a silver carving knife before jumping out of one of the Club's second-floor windows.

However, it isn't his ghost who haunts the Club.

The Lady was a Tramp

The real ghost story concerns an old gentleman who belonged to the Club, and who frequently enjoyed the company of a local lady of the night. He would tell his wife he was going out to the Club to hang with his homeboys, and then he would take a horse-drawn carriage a little farther down Hollis Street to the red-light district.

Once there, he would climb up to a third-floor walk-up and the room of a lady with whom he enjoyed spending time and money, although they never left her bedroom.

Afterwards the man would make his way to the Halifax Club and sit in silence, sipping a cup of strong port while puffing on a pipe full of less-than-fragrant Latakia pipe tobacco, the pungent aroma guaranteeing him a wide circle of comfortable solitude. He rarely spoke during these evening vigils. He just sat there smiling to himself, reliving his latest sordid adventure with his lady friend.

Then one night the port and tobacco caught up with him.

He passed out in the arms of his love-for-hire, which wasn't uncommon. However this time he decided to stop breathing, which had never happened before. His heart gave out and he died in a rented bed.

She was deeply worried about the impending scandal. She worried it would be bad for her business. After all, several other of her patrons frequented the Halifax Club. It would not do for the story of this man to get out into the realm of common knowledge.

Thinking quickly, the young woman called for the Halifax Club's house steward who hastily rounded up an emergency task group of patrons known for their discretion. They made their way down Hollis Street carrying the old boy's freshly dressed body, and they placed his corpse upon the steps of the Halifax Club. It was quite a clever plan.

Rather than try to cover up the old man's shenanigans, they decided perhaps it would be better if it appeared he had simply keeled over on his way into the club.

I have not been able to find any sort of newspaper reference to this particular story, which goes to show just how effective a cover-up it really was. To this day, members of the Halifax Club swear they can still occasionally smell the malodorous aroma of the old boy's pungent tobacco drifting through the halls of the Halifax Club.

However, the story does not end here.

The Lady Falls Down

It was only recently that I first came across a rather juicy addendum to this story in the pages of our wonderful local weekly newspaper, *The Coast*. According to the article's author, Jacob Boon, the story of the gentleman's heart attack did *not* end where everyone thinks it did.

According to the tour guide at the Halifax Club, the group of concerned patrons who had carried the old boy's body back to the steps of the club had then returned to the third-floor walk-up, where they forced their way back into the woman's bedroom. After a brief struggle they threw her out of her third-floor window and she crashed to her death in the street below.

Sadly, this rather sordid little story makes an awful lot of sense.

The men in question apparently felt this rude and unexpected disposal was the very best way to ensure the woman's future discretion. A dead woman would certainly not be unable to embarrass the nineteenth-century patrons of the prestigious Club.

Again, whether this side of the story is true or not, I cannot in all honesty tell you—but as I said, it makes an awful lot of sense.

I looked into this part of the story and I am afraid I was unable to find any sort of reference to either of these deaths. In truth, it wasn't really the sort of news item that would warrant much in the way of newspaper coverage back then. Still, given the way people felt back then about keeping up appearances and maintaining a socially acceptable reputation, it wouldn't surprise me if both stories were true.

47: More Ghost Stories Than You Can Shake a Pitchfork At!

44°34'51.4"N 63°27'30.5"W

THIS IS ONE OF THE most inaccessible haunted Nova Scotia locations that I am going to list for you here in this book. When I first visited Devils Island it was by a helicopter that a friend of mine had chartered for us. There were only a couple of people living on the island at the time: an artist and his wife, and a large German shepherd by the name of Thor.

These two people lived on Devils Island by themselves, serving as caretakers. Supplies had to be flown in or transported by dory. Still, both of them seemed to enjoy the solitude. They were the last two people to live upon that tiny secluded island.

You cannot easily see Devils Island from the Halifax side of the harbour because it is crouched in the shadow of the far larger McNabs Island. You need to travel to the far edges of Dartmouth to get a good look at it; a kilometre and a half from Hartland Point.

The owner of the island, noted Halifax historian and flea-market baron Bill Mont, has told me many times that Devils Island is one of the most haunted locations in Nova Scotia, so I believe it would be a very bad idea to leave this location out of the book.

Let me start out by telling you a little bit about the history of Devils Island.

Back in 1711, French engineer Jean Delabat, while scouting out the region in hopes of finding a suitable location for a French settlement, drew up a map of the entrance to Halifax Harbour to show his superiors. In the end, the French government decided the harbour was far too deep and open for any sort of a settlement, so they left it to the British.

Delabat had called the little island Île Verte due to the heavy woods that dominated it, and when the British finally did settle in Halifax they renamed Île Verte the far-more-prosaic Wood Island. That name lasted a short while until local authorities deeded the property to British sea captain John Rous and it became known simply as Rous Island. Eventually, the story goes, the island was sold again, this time to a Frenchman by the name of Duvall. It became known as Duvalls Island, which eventually mumbled its way down into what the island is now known as: Devils Island.

In 1830, Andrew Henneberry, whose lease on McNabs Island had expired, moved and settled upon Devils Island. Shortly afterwards, Thomas Edwards and several of his brothers also moved to Devils Island. By 1850 there were three houses and a small school upon the island, and by 1901 the tiny island village had grown into eighteen houses.

In 1883 a lifesaving station was set up along with a crew of hardy dorymen who kept a careful watch for foundering ships. If there were any vessels in trouble the crew would row out and give what aid they could, either by helping to repair the vessel or more as likely rowing the shipwrecked sailors back to the safety of Devils Island and leaving the stricken ship to sink into the sea.

In 1914 the First World War began in Europe and the young men of the island enlisted and sailed away. Others grew tired of island life and simply moved away. Eventually, the small village became a town of lonely ghosts. Nowadays no one lives upon this little island, not even a caretaker. An automated lighthouse is the only sign of life upon this desolate island.

"To the Devil with it," the last man was reported to say as he left Devils Island.

The Tales of Devils Island

In the late 1920s, famed Nova Scotia folklore collector Helen Creighton began to research the stories behind Devils Island. At least once a week she would walk down to the Hartland Point shoreline and wave towards Devils Island. The family that lived on the island, the Henneberrys, learned to keep watch for her and they would row out in a dory and row her back to the island for a visit. Sometimes she arrived with an old-style tape-recording device, pushing it along in a big old wheelbarrow. Other times she just showed up with a notepad.

I love that image. I can picture her out there gathering stories, like a fisherman out early in the morning to trawl the waters for a wet harvest. If you were out there and saw this woman pushing a wheelbarrow you might think her dotty or possibly pity her, but her words and stories have lasted for over fifty years. Her book, *Bluenose Ghosts*, still continues to be read across the world.

One of my favourite Devils Island stories was told to me this way by an old fisherman named Allison who told me that he had first read it in the pages of *Bluenose Ghosts*. Now, I have read *Bluenose Ghosts* from cover to cover, and although Helen Creighton does relate a little about this story, old Allison added an awful lot to it along the way.

The Tale of Allison

"My name's Allison," the old fellow told me. "And you might feel yourself wanting to giggle to hear a man with a girl's name, but I was named after my daddy. Back then Allison was a name for a boy, and that's the honest truth of it."

He stood there and grinned at me like he was daring me to laugh, only I did not have the nerve.

"Well sir, it was my daddy who told me this tale and the way he told it to me was this way. He told me that one morning old Casper Henneberry was out to a dance on Devils Island and he told this story to a bunch of his buddies."

"Casper?" I asked, interrupting. "Like the ghost?"

"I said Gaspar," Allison replied. "Are you listening or not?"

I assured him I was, and I resolved to remain quiet for the rest of the story. I didn't think I was going to hear the rest of it any other way.

"Old Gaspar was saying his goodbyes," Allison went on. "He told his friends they were all invited to a wake next week.

'Whose wake are we invited to?' one friend asked. 'A wake means death, and I haven't heard of anyone dying lately.'

'It is to be my own wake,' Gaspar told them. 'I don't know when it is coming but I know that it is coming soon.'

The group grew a little quiet at this news.

'Has the doctor given you some piece of bad news?' one of Gaspar's closest friends asked. 'Has the crab bit you with the cancer?'

'No sir,' Gaspar replied. 'It wasn't no doctor that told me this news.'

'Well then who was it that told you?'

'It was the Devil himself what told me to go and say my goodbyes,' Gaspar replied. 'I saw him just last night when I was coming up from the beach.'

'What did he look like?' one of his friends asked. 'Did he have them cloven feet and a tail and horns?'

'Well, if you have to know,' Gaspar said, 'he looked just exactly like a big walking halibut, one of the flattest and ugliest fish in the sea.'

'A giant halibut?' one of his friends asked with a sly fishhook-sort-of grin. 'Did you think to invite him in for dinner?'

'I bet you all a solid silver dollar the old fish's breath smelled of rum spirits,' another friend said. 'And I bet you another solid silver dollar that old Gaspar's breath smelled twice as bad.'

'This weren't no rum spirit,' Gaspar said, with a stubborn shake of his curly grey head. 'It were a halibut, nearly seven feet tall and standing on two stumpy little legs and his eyes were so mean and cold that I knew deep down inside of my soul that this was the Devil for certain sure.'

The tone of Gaspar's voice left no room for giggling. They could see the man was speaking what he believed to be the truth and they took him at his word.

'Why a halibut?' one friend asked. 'Isn't that supposed to be some sort of a holy fish?'

'Give that man both of your silver dollars,' Gaspar said. 'A halibut *is* a holy fish, which is why you will find so many halibuts sizzling in frying pans every Fish Friday.'

'So what was the Devil doing dressed up as a halibut?'

'The way I figure it, the whole idea struck the old goat as funny, him wearing a mackerel like he was.' Gaspar explained. 'It was his version of a trick-or-treat prank, if you know what I mean.'

'So, what all did he tell you?' one friend asked. 'Did he try and bargain for your soul?'

'No bargain was ever discussed,' Gaspar said. 'He just told me he was glad he had bumped into me and he was going to be seeing me one more time out there on the sea. He said I was going to catch my very best load of fish come tomorrow and by sundown I would have sailed my last dory load back home.'

'What else did he say?'

'He said nothing else. He just vanished in a cloud of smoke that smelled of fish oil and brimstone,' Gaspar said. 'I haven't been able to get the stink out of the house since.'

'So what are you going to do about it?' one friend asked. 'Are you staying ashore, then?'

Gaspar shook his head.

'I have been fishing these waters for sixty long years and I sure ain't going to let any old Devil steer me any different,' Gaspar said.

'There is a tide running tomorrow and I intend to be running with it. I'll be home with a dory full of fresh-caught fish by sundown, or my name isn't Gaspar Henneberry.'"

"What happened then?" I asked, interrupting Allison in spite of my inner promise to stay quiet.

"Does your nose ever hurt you from butting it into a story so hard?" Allison asked me back. "Just hush up and I will finish telling this story straight on through."

So I shut up again, which is really the very best thing to do when you are trying your best to listen to a story you really want to hear.

"Well, there really isn't all that much more to tell," Allison said. "The very next morning Gaspar was as good as word. There was a tide running and he was running with it; by sundown he came back on home with a dory full of fresh-caught halibut, some of the biggest and ugliest fish you have ever seen. Old Gaspar was with them, but he was stone-cold dead with his head hanging down over the side of his dory looking for all the world like somebody had clubbed him silly."

"Was it the Devil?" I asked.

"How should I know?" Allison said. "Some fellows I know believe Allison had made himself that deal he said he hadn't, bargaining with the Devil for his soul in exchange for a dory load of fresh-caught fish."

"Do you think that's true?"

He fixed me with a sharp look.

"How should I know?" Allison repeated. "Some other fellows tell this story and it ends with them finding Allison's body, minus a head—as if he had run into somebody with an awfully mean grudge. Maybe his heart had just gave out cold. Sixty years of hard fishing on open water will do that to a man, as sure as sin."

"Well what do you figure?" I asked.

Allison looked out over the water and thought for a moment.

"I figure I have talked myself dry," Allison said. "And I am heading for the nearest tavern. If you don't follow me in and pay me for the trouble of telling you this story with a nice, tall, cold glass of ale, then to the Devil with you and all your storytelling ways."

So that's what we did.

48: The Last Bow of the Ghost Light
44.6460° N, 63.5741° W

ANY VISIT TO THE HALIFAX region would not be complete without a trip to Neptune Theatre, Halifax's largest live theatre.

Surprisingly enough, the Neptune Theatre actually has its very own ghost story. In fact, it has several—and although I have already told one of these stories in my earlier collection *Halifax Haunts*, there are several others available and I have this one in particular I want to share with you shortly.

But first, let me tell you a bit about the history of Neptune.

The building was originally home to the Strand Theatre and was designed by Nova Scotia's very first professional architect, Andrew Cobb. The Strand was known worldwide as the very first vaudeville house to be specifically constructed to be a full-sized theatre.

However, following a mysterious fire in 1926, the Strand Theatre briefly reopened as a cinema before the Wall Street Crash of 1929 closed its doors. At the time it was whispered that a local bawdy house had opened above the cinema, but that rather sordid detail has not been verified. The theatre reopened again as the Garrick Repertory Theatre and then, in 1963, the Neptune Theatre was finally born.

I have been to Neptune many times as a theatre spectator. I have also performed several times as a storyteller, and although I have never seen any sort of ghost in this theatre—unless maybe you count Charles Dickens's ghosts of Christmas Past, Present, and Future, or maybe Hamlet's dead daddy—I can assure you there are an awful lot of stories about the strange and haunted goings-on at Neptune Theatre.

Helena Marriott, head of Neptune's wardrobe department, and Sandra Hum, a wardrobe mistress, will tell you how a Neptune seamstress saw a dead-eyed man all dressed in black sitting on a heap of fabric. These ladies will also tell you how many coloured industrial-sized cones of sewing thread leaped off a nearby shelf and flew across the crowded sewing room to strike another seamstress square in the forehead.

"They did not just topple off the shelf," Marriott reported in a CBC live broadcast. "They actually arced across the room as if they were being thrown."

However, this is not the story I wish to share with you. The story I am going tell you involves Neptune Theatre's ghost light.

So, what is a ghost light?

A ghost light is an actual lamp that is left burning on the stage after everyone has gone home for the evening. This is a custom followed by live theatres all across North America. The reason behind this practice is safety; a precaution for any worker who might be left behind after the establishment's doors close. A light is left burning so said hapless employee does not accidentally stumble off of the main stage in the darkness and break a leg, or worse yet, their neck.

However, if you ask any actor—and as you might know, actors are some of the most superstitious creatures that walk the face of this earth—they will tell you that in addition to the practical reason, there is also a strong and powerful supernatural reason for leaving a ghost light burning upon a darkened stage.

Plenty of theatre actors believe their theatres are haunted by the ghosts of old actors who simply refuse to leave the stage after they have passed away. To take their final bow, as it were. The light is left on to comfort them, and to keep them fascinated by its glimmer and out of trouble.

A Neptune actor named Charles stayed behind to clean up after an evening performance one night. He wasn't a star, just a working actor, and the cleaning job was just another way of putting bread upon his table. It helped to pay the bills.

While he was cleaning up, he spotted a figure standing up on the stage, silhouetted in the shimmer of the ghost lamp. Or rather he saw the shadow of a figure in the halo of the ghost lamp. The shadow was tall and lean and dark-looking, and it appeared to be wearing a long, dark dovetailed dining jacket.

"W-who are you?" Charles asked, his voice cracking with unexpected terror and a very real kind of stage fright. "Speak, I tell you. Speak!"

Only that shadow of a figure would not speak a single syllable. The shadow just stood there looking to its left and right as if it— and there was no other pronoun Charles could readily conjure except for "it"—as if it could not find just exactly what it was looking for.

And then the eerie and mysterious shadow began to dance a stomping jig Charles immediately recognized as an old-time vaudeville dance that had once been called a buck-and-a-wing. It was the sort of a happy kind of dance that in any other circumstance would have brought a smile to Charles's face…only he wasn't smiling. That dancing shadow was way too eerie a sight for Charles to want to crack a grin at, no matter how much he felt he ought to.

Now, ordinarily a dance like that would have sounded like the crackle of popcorn and tap shoes, but all Charles could hear was the sound of a gravedigger's spade shovelling freshly turned dirt onto a cheaply painted pine casket. Charles stood there in the shadows of the empty auditorium, not knowing what to do. He found himself absurdly wishing he knew his line.

And then it came to him: all at once, Charles knew just what the shadow was waiting for. He raised his hands up—slowly, slowly, slowly. Charles stood there, holding his breath without even realizing he was holding it, his two hands held out in front of him in mid-air, about a foot apart, as if he were trying to demonstrate just how large a fish had slipped his line.

And then Charles began to clap.

His first claps were soft, and then they began to build in intensity like the sound of a horse, galloping down a hard paved hill. As Charles clapped the room filled with more ghostly shadows of a huge audience; more bodies than Neptune Theatre had ever held. They were all thunderously applauding the ghostly shadow dancer.

The shadow on stage bowed slowly, down and down until it sunk into a lonely spot on the floor. Then the shadow was gone.

The audience was gone as well.

Charles was standing alone in a dark room full of empty theatre seats, lit only by the flickering light of the ghost lamp on stage.

"Encore?" Charles softly whispered, with only the slightest trace of hesitation hidden in his voice. "Encore? Encore?"

49: Oscar Wilde Has His Final Say
44°38'27.0"N 63°34'16.2"W

IN THE YEAR 1887 WHILE Buffalo Bill's Travelling Wild West Show was touring Europe—and Thomas Edison was arm-wrestling Nikola Tesla for control of the North-American power industry—noted Irish author Oscar Fingal O'Flahertie Wills Wilde (October 16, 1854—November 30, 1900) completed a two-part novella entitled *The Canterville Ghost.* It told the story of an American family that moved to an English castle haunted by the ghost of a dead nobleman who had reportedly killed his wife and was subsequently starved to death in punishment by his wife's brothers—which is a good reason not to peeve off your in-laws!

Three years later, Oscar Wilde wrote the novel he would become most famous for, *The Picture of Dorian Grey,* a Faust-like story of young man who trades his soul for the gift of immortality, given to him in the form of a portrait that shows all signs of age and sinful living for him, while he continues maintaining the appearance of seemingly endless youth.

Since then, both stories have been adapted for stage and screen many times over. It is interesting to note how deeply each of these stories were rooted in Gothic supernaturalism. It appears Oscar was quite at home in the heart of a good old-fashioned ghost story.

The Waverley Inn

The Waverley Inn was originally built in 1865 under the guiding hand of a prosperous Halifax dry-goods merchant by the name of Edward W. Chipman and his wife, Mahala Jane Northrup (or Maria, according to some historical sources). The Chipman family home was built in a year, which was making good time for nineteenth-century construction. Apparently Edward would not put up with any sort of delay: Mahala had parties to throw.

Mahala was well known back then for the extravagant dances, parties, and impromptu bashes she loved to host. The parties were always well attended, with appearances from local celebrities, highly ranked British officers, and well-to-do private citizens. The house was described as being "in the style, both in regards to size and decoration, more like a palace than any sort of private residence."

Unfortunately, due to lavish overspending and an unforeseen setback in his dry-goods business, Edward W. Chipman was suddenly and unexpectedly forced to sell his business for the best offer he could get, which came by way of a sheriff's auction and a bid from Halifax real-estate speculator Patrick Costin.

The Chipmans left town shortly afterward, headed west, eventually settling in St. Paul, Minnesota. Meanwhile, back in Halifax, Patrick Costin happily handed over ownership of the Chipman mansion for approximately $14,000 to a pair of canny spinster sisters, Sarah and Jane Romans, who aimed to build upon their success running their father's inn, which was also known as the Waverley Inn.

Sarah and Jane commissioned the addition of a new wing on the rear of the Chipman house, and moved in. They began taking in guests as of October of 1876. Within a short time, they had established an immaculate reputation as being a fine place to spend the evening.

Which brings us to Oscar Wilde, who stayed at the Waverley Inn on the first few nights of his 1882 tour of North America. Oscar was described as a very flamboyant character, fond of wearing green velvet pantaloons and gold buckle shoes—gaudy apparel, even for that day and age. For a sizable honorarium, Oscar would come to your home and entertain your family and guests. He was an old-style busker as well as an author, and by all reports an accomplished performer.

Unfortunately, his public performances were poorly received by Haligonians, in spite of the lavishly decorated stage that had been set up at the Halifax Academy of Music. The stage was set with fine furniture that had been begged, borrowed, and donated by several local businesses, as well as several exotic animal skins and, oddly enough, a tiny stuffed Chinese pug.

The room was filled to capacity with an audience who had happily paid the seventy-five-cent admission fee, a princely sum back in the nineteenth century. Even though Oscar hadn't yet written any of the books and plays he would eventually became famous for, he already had a reputation for being a bit of a wild card; people had gone to his performance expecting some sort of scandalous behaviour.

Sadly, the speech Oscar had prepared was on the Aesthetic Movement in Europe. As he droned on and on about the choice of furnishings, rug work, and wallpaper, some people actually stood up and walked out. Oscar's talk was panned in the local newspaper.

Even though he left Halifax under a cloud of disappointment, he earnestly promised the management of the Waverly Inn that he would someday return.

According to folks who have stayed at the inn over the years, the author was as good as his word.

Oscar Wilde's ghost continues to haunt the building over one hundred years later. Witnesses describe his ghost as being garishly dressed. He is often seen standing, reading a book. He was a tall man and probably found it uncomfortable to hunker down for too long in a normal-sized chair. The owners of the Waverley Inn have further preserved the author's memory by naming one of the rooms after him. Visitors swear they have seen his ghost standing at the doorway to the Oscar Wilde room.

He hasn't terrified anyone to all reports; he is more of a friendly sort of a presence, often detected in those dark and lonely wolf hours that follow the stroke of midnight. You can still rent room 122, where he reportedly stayed. Just ask for the Wilde Room. You will know it by the large portrait of Oscar that hangs upon the rose-print wallpaper. Only be warned: you have to book well in advance.

Oscar can still draw a crowd, I guess.

50: The Pirate Ghost of Point Pleasant Park
44°37'22"N 63°34'9"W

RIGHT OFF THE BAT, POINT Pleasant Park is a wonderful spot to go hiking and picnicking and walking down by the beach. You can take in an outdoor play, courtesy of Shakespeare by the Sea. You can visit several old historic sites including a fortress and a huge round Martello Tower named after the Prince of Wales.

When I first came to live in Halifax I was warned by several people that the body of a young man had been found in those deep woods, tied upright between the trunks of two trees, and badly mutilated. I don't really know if that story is true or just an urban myth, but right away my imagination started revolving around the park.

Later on I was employed as a tour-bus storyteller and I was given a ghost story about a young fellow named Jordan who had been hanged on Black Rock Beach. I actually retold that very same story in my collection *Haunted Harbours: Ghost Stories From Old Nova Scotia*. It was a sweet and sort of melancholy story.

Further research unearthed the truth of the matter. The "Jordan" in the story actually referred to Edward Jordan: a fierce and feared pirate who was hanged on Black Rock Beach. In truth, his story was neither sweet nor melancholy.

Now sit down and let me tell it to you.

The whole thing started out on July 17, 1809, when Captain John Stairs of the schooner *The Three Sisters* set sail from Halifax Harbour. He had a crew consisting of John Kelly (first mate), Thomas Heath (pilot), and Benjamin Matthews and John Tremain (seamen). The schooner was bound for Percé, Quebec, where they intended to pick up a cargo of dried fish.

There was a sixth sailor as well, and that was Edward Jordan, who was accompanied by his wife, Margaret Jordan, and their four children—three girls and one boy.

The trip to Percé was routine. *The Three Sisters* arrived there on September 10, 1809, picked up her cargo of dried fish, and headed back out to sea. Three days later the trouble began.

The schooner was sailing between Cape Canso and Whitehead. Captain Smith was belowdeck in his cabin, fetching his quadrant to shoot the sun in order to check the ship's latitude. Heath, the pilot, was with him, awaiting his captain's instructions. Suddenly the captain looked up from the pages of his chart book and saw Edward Jordan with a pistol in his hand.

Jordan fired, and the pistol ball carved a channel along Captain Stairs's nose and face, before striking Heath in the chest.

"My God, I am killed," Heath said, falling to his knees, crawling towards the cabin hatch, and up the stairs toward the deck. Jordan calmly followed him, laughing at the man's obvious distress.

Taking advantage of the moment, Captain Stairs dove for the pair of pistols he kept stored in his chest, however when he opened the chest he was shocked to see that someone had already stolen the pistols. He was searching for his cutlass when he heard several shots fired up on deck.

He turned towards the cabin hatch and Jordan met him at the top of the staircase with an axe in his right hand and the pistol in his left.

"Kelly!" the captain called out for his first mate as he grappled with Jordan. The pistol went overboard followed by the axe. The captain was fighting in sheer terror, because he could see Heath's body lying on the deck, shot full of holes. Jordan pulled free and picked up another axe and struck down Benjamin Matthew, who had turned up just in time to be hacked a half dozen times with Jordan's axe. Jordan's wife appeared at his side.

"KELLY!" the captain called out again.

"Kelly, is it?" Margaret Jordan jeered, striking the Captain on the back of his skull with the shaft of a long-handled boat hook.

The captain went down and Margaret stepped over him to pummel Matthew's dying body, just in case her husband Edward needed any help. That was all the chance Captain Stairs needed. He dragged a ship's hatch over to the railing and jumped over the side with the door in his arms.

"Let him go," Jordan ordered. "He won't stand a chance in this frigid water."

Meanwhile, throughout the whole battle, First Mate John Kelly had stood quietly at the wheel. He had already made his decision and struck a deal with the Jordans to help them with the mutiny and seize The Three Sisters.

"He didn't know it was bath night, now did he?" Kelly asked Jordan, laughing out loud.

Only Captain Stairs was made out of tougher material than Edward, Margaret, or Kelly could guess. Hours later, still clinging to the hatch door that served as a makeshift raft, Captain Stairs was rescued by a passing American schooner.

Several days later, the British military schooner Cuttle came alongside The Three Sisters and arrested Edward and Margaret Jordan, who had already parted ways with John Kelly. Jordan was returned to Halifax, where he would stand trial for murder, mutiny, and piracy.

On January 10, 1810, the verdicts were returned: John Kelly was pardoned, as was Margaret Jordan. The court just did not want the responsibility of hanging a mother of four young children. Edward Jordan, however, was not so lucky. The jury spent a scant sixty minutes deciding his fate.

"You, Edward Jordan, shall be taken to the place whence you came, and there to be hanged by the neck until you are dead. May God Almighty have mercy upon your soul," the judge declared.

Edward Jordan was hanged on November 23, 1810, at Freshwater Bridge. There is a little park there at the end Barrington Street where it runs into Inglis Street. A crowd gathered, and people applauded when he went through the trapdoor. His one claim to fame was that he was the very first "pirate" to be hung in Canada.

His last words were: "God have mercy upon me. What will happen to my poor children?"

Afterwards, his body was taken to Black Rock Beach where it was coated with tar, caged, and gibbeted. His dangling tar-blackened corpse could serve as a warning for any would-be malefactors who sailed into Halifax Harbour. His remains hung there for nearly thirty years before finally being taken down.

People still stay that on certain calm nights you can hear the *clunk* of the trapdoor dropping beneath Edward Jordan's noosed body. Eyewitnesses have also reported seeing his ghost walking along the shore of Black Rock Beach, perhaps searching for his long-lost wife and children.

Oddly enough, his skull has been kept as a curio in the Nova Scotia Museum on Summer Street, and some people have also reported seeing the ghost of Edward Jordan walking the halls of the museum.

The fellow really gets around, doesn't he?

Other Books by Steve Vernon

Haunted Harbours:
Ghost Stories from Old Nova Scotia

Wicked Woods:
Ghost Stories from Old New Brunswick

Halifax Haunts:
Exploring the City's Spookiest Space

Maritime Monsters:
A Field Guide

The Lunenburg Werewolf
and Other Stories of the Supernatural

Sinking Deeper
Or, My Questionable (Possibly Heroic) Decision
to Invent a Sea Monster

Maritime Murder:
Deadly Crimes from the Buried Past